THE FOURTH LEVEL
SON OF RA
BOOK FIVE

NICHOLAS HUNTLEY

"Presently, details of the room emerged slowly from the mist, strange animals, statues and gold – everywhere the glint of gold... and when Lord Carnarvon, unable to stand in suspense any longer, inquired anxiously, 'Can you see anything?' it was all I could do to get out the words, 'Yes, wonderful things.'"

– Howard Carter

Act 1, Scene 1

The amber meld of the sun dawned from over the Atlas Mountains like the fireball it felt to be. The fine grains of the desert sand at its base began to bake in their Martian red colors and induce a heat haze mirage of warm air. The dawn horizon became a mesh of the coldness of the night sky met with the orange warmth of the sunrise hue. Daylight rolled across the desert hills and brought light onto this side of the world once again.

Sunlight lifted the shadows along the red stone walls of the old city where cars and apartment buildings were kept out to preserve the rich and ancient history of Marrakesh. Inside the older town, the echoes of the *al-Fajr* filled every alleyway and arcade between the tanned stone huts and shops that structured the medina. From above, the old city was like a labyrinth with the open space of *Jemaa el-Fnaa*, a marketplace buzzling with movement and interest.

Moroccans and tourists alike swarmed around in opposing directions in the commercial square of the old city whilst men pitted their goods to the masses, competing with one another for in another day's hard work. Caravans travelled through and left to go deeper into the routes of the old city where more shops could be found beneath the alleyways shaded by ceiling blinds. The screams of children playing met with the shouts of hagglers created a unique ambience of the Middle East alongside the chatter of wind chimes and ringing of bicycle bells.

A vase shattered against a sandy road where one of the merchant's sons dropped a ceramic jar loaded with water. The water induced a splash that fell upon the surrounding dry ground, causing the boy to jump in fear and look to his father as he yelled at him. The water spread from where it landed and began to roll down the slanted street. It trickled down and began to enter past the bars of a basement window of a building.

The water slipped through the slits and started to trickle down into the darkened sublevel of the room on the other side. Each drop made its freefall in turns, creating a distinctive and rhythmic dripping sound that echoed through the silenced voice in the room.

"Is it raining outside," asked a young male voice in a Yorkshire accent.

"Don't be daft," an older voice with a Londoner accent replied. "Can't you see the sun shining through the bars? It's morning."

"No, I can't see the sun because as a matter of fact," the younger character remarked, "you're the one facing the window."

"Oh, very well," the other whispered, looking up and towards the window.

The older man had light blue eyes that cringed as he looked towards the brightness in contrast to the darkness of the chamber he was in. He endured the difference of light and could see sandaled feet and robed characters passing along the street. He then tilted his head down and looked at his brown leather boots. He gave a sigh and felt a tear of sweat roll down the side of his face from his steel white hair.

"Are you sure help is on the way?" the younger character asked as he leaned up, touching the rear of the head of his employer.

"Of course," the older gentleman scoffed, twitching his upper lip to brush his moustache, "show a little patience. I sent my best woman on the case."

• •

"Hello?" a soft-voiced English accent asked, knocking on the tall door of a small Moroccan Kasbah in the middle of the old town.

The doors began to open, revealing a tall and wide muscular figure in a fine, reddish-pink open-collar dress shirt underneath a fine-pressed magenta suit. He had dark tanned skin and a frown that dropped his forehead and eyebrows over his eyes. His forehead of which was elongated and stuck out. His head was also round and he was bald. The man wasn't alone. To his left was an accomplice in a similar suit, but this man was shorter and skinnier. He had a thin beard with short black hair. His open-collar dress shirt revealed a tuff of chest hair alongside a gold chain necklace. He also wore sunglasses that weren't tinted enough to reveal his eyes and thick eyebrows from behind. Each of them had an earpiece that crawled up the side of their neck and came into their right ears.

The two spoke in Arabic to each other before they stepped towards the small woman. She wore a dress over her roundish body. She also had a briefcase in her hands. A scarf was wrapped over her head, leaving only her face and hands visible.

"The boss wants to see you," the skinnier man said, approaching her with a toothy smile. "Right this way, miss."

The woman entered the building and carefully made her way forward with suspicion. A red carpet covered the terracotta tiles of the entrance. She stepped forward, looking around the richly decorated home and travelled to where there were two more guards dressed alike in the same suits. The guards opened another pair of doors for her.

Light flowed in from outside as behind the doors was revealed a marvelous courtyard garden with a pool fountain in the middle and various shrubs and flora around the sides. The sun beamed down into the Andalusian home. The woman made her way around the fountain to where she saw a man in a chair at a small table, reading a newspaper.

"Mrs. Quinn, I presume," the man said in a Londoner accent.

Mavis looked at him. He was dressed differently from the others. He had a white suit with a silver open-collar shirt. He also had thin receding black hair and a fine jawline despite appearing to be quite young. Lastly, he also wore a gold wristwatch on his left wrist.

"I presume that this is my money, my dear," the man said, closing his newspaper and setting it on the table.

Mavis' hand trembled at the handle of the briefcase. Three guards, including the two that let her in, approached from behind. An additional two guards made their appearance behind their boss, in front of some doors going inside the *riad*. Mavis could also see some additional guards on the balconies above. Behind the boss, on a pedestal was a strange stone-like item on a pillow underneath a glass case.

"I am here to negotiate the release of Mr. Cabernet and Mr. Southern," Mavis said.

The boss continued to smile to her.

"Mrs. Quinn, the release of Mr. Cabernet was already negotiated with Mr. Huxley. Now, if you'd be so kind to hand over the briefcase with our unmarked bills…"

The larger enforcer stepped over to Mavis and took the briefcase from her hand with ease and no resistance. He took the briefcase and set it down on the table near the boss.

"If I do not have my five million, Mrs. Quinn," the boss said, "I'm going to be very, very angry."

The man unlatched the locks of the briefcase and then gently opened it. Mavis looked anxiously as the man opened the case, looking inside and dropping his smile. Inside, there were rows of Euros piled overtop. The man began to giggle and then laughed. He turned to Mavis with open arms.

"Ma'am, you are too nice!" the man shouted, laughing some more. "Mahmoud, get the wine! Iro, release the prisoners, will you?"

The man continued to laugh as Mavis stood where she was, hands at her lap as wine glasses were brought over with a wide bottle of rosé wine. Mavis appeared shy as she stood silent, looking around and carefully examining the location as some guards dispersed. She was given a glass to hold and a guard poured her some of the wine. The boss took a glass and had some wine poured for himself too.

"Cheers!" the man said, bringing their glasses together.

The two glasses clinked together before the man parted from her, still giggling to himself before he downed a large portion of the wine. Mavis sipped hers as her eyes met the open briefcase. The bills shook, but nobody but her noticed. They then shook again.

"Huh?" the larger enforcer questioned, looking at the bills.

The boss looked at the bills when a quad-drone jumped out and smashed him in the face, hitting him on the nose. The man swore in Arabic and then tried to swat the machine as it flew up and out of the way. Several guards drew their pistols and started to open fire. Mavis attempted to flee, but the large enforcer hugged her and restrained her as she brought her up. She resisted and spilt wine on the floor. Her feet waved around in the air.

"You dishonorable dog!" the man yelled, leaning over with his hands to his bloodied nose. "Shoot down that toy!"

The drone dodged the gunfire before a red light on the middle started to beep. The beeping gained pace, prompting Mavis to bring her foot up and kick the enforcer in the groins. He yelled out and let her go. She then rushed away and hid behind a large potted plant. The drone then discharged arcs of electricity out and towards each guard, electrocuting them momentarily before they fell over subdued.

The boss was unaffected as he hid under a table. He looked around before removing his hand from his nose. He reached into his suit, but Mavis was quick to react as she threw her wine glass at him, smashing itself on his head and causing him to fall over. Mavis then stood up and in a panic, dashed into the building.

"We must hurry," she said to the drone as it followed her.

The two entered the home. She began to run forward and around a corner where the coast was clear. She then started to dash forward to where she saw Iro, the bald and skinny guard disappear off to.

Mavis dashed over to the other side when the doors burst open with a man holding a flamethrower. He focused his attention on the drone flying above, causing a stream of flames to spew out and upwards. Mavis ducked and fled from the flames, regrouping with the drone at the end of the hall as they continued forward. All sorts of flammable material in the corridor caught on fire. Mavis disappeared down a set of stairwells in the room she was now in, finding herself in another corridor with barrels of liquor on the right-side.

The passageway was simple with a door on the other end. Mavis quickly made her way forward with the quadcopter close. She opened the medieval door and entered inside, seeing Iro ahead with keys in-hand as he was about to open the door.

Iro turned to her and tried to draw a pistol from his jacket, but the drone was quick to discharge another arc into him, stunning him and causing him to drop both the pistol and keys. Mavis then walked over, picked up an expensive-looking vase on a stand, and smashed it into the man, knocking him out.

Charlemagne's ears twitched as he heard the commotion coming from the other side of the room. He stamped his feet, while his partner heard the noise too.

"We're in here!" Charlemagne shouted.

The two of them listened to the sound of the door unlocking, and felt the breeze come through the door as it opened. The drone entered first before Mavis entered to untie their ties.

"Well, it's about time," Southern remarked as he was untied.

"We always had faith in you, love," Charlemagne commended. "Quickly, we have to get the relic before it's too late."

Charlemagne stood up and led the team out the door. Each of them ran out with him to the room adjacent.

"Johnathan, take that pistol," Charlemagne said to his partner, pointing at the gun on the floor. "Take point."

"Yes, Mr. Cabernet," Johnathan replied, taking the gun and making sure it was loaded before he led the team.

The four of them walked down the wine corridor and made it upstairs.

"Goodness, look at the entrance you've made," Charlemagne remarked as he looked around. "Where's the relic? Do you know? He brought it with him when we were captured."

"I saw it in the garden," Mavis replied. "It was on a pedestal."

The drone and Johnathan went forward, down the corridor and back into the garden where the other guards were still unconscious. An additional two guards had turned up, while the boss had woken up and held his hand at a door. He looked over to Charlemagne and his party as they arrived.

"Kill them!" the man shouted.

Johnathan immediately fired his gun at the shins of the two other guard, causing them to collapse in pain. The boss then attempted to escape through the door, but it wouldn't open for him. He instead looked over to Charlemagne and then the glass case where the relic was. Charlemagne did the same, looking to him and then the relic. Charlemagne and the boss rushed over to the pedestal. Johnathan tried to fire at the man beforehand, but he missed and raised his gun up with caution as Charlemagne came into the line of fire.

The man beat Charlemagne to the relic, pulling over the glass case and then grabbing the relic into his hands before he ran off.

"After him!" Charlemagne shouted, leading them.

Johnathan immediately dashed forward with Mavis and the drone. Charlemagne led them to the exit of the building and then onto the streets of Marrakesh where the boss was making escape through the crowds of people. Johnathan met up with Charlemagne, put the pistol away, and then continued forward, shoving past people. Mavis met up with Charlemagne and caught her breath, waving her hand to Charlemagne to leave her behind.

"I will... stay here... in case he... comes back," Mavis panted.

"Good idea," Charlemagne replied. "Lucky, stay here and protect Mrs. Quinn."

The drone, Lucky, maintained its position as Charlemagne went forward into the crowd. He could see Johnathan ahead who could see the boss moving around. The boss turned a corner and continued downwards as they approached the market square.

Charlemagne stopped as he got to the entrance, tracing eyes from Johnathan to the collect where he stood out due to his violent and rash movement. Johnathan continued forward but began to lose him in the crowds of vendors and shoppers. He spun around, losing him definitely as there were too many people that overwhelmed his eyes. Charlemagne caught up with him and looked around.

"Do you see him? Where'd he go?" Charlemagne questioned.

"I- I don't know," Johnathan replied.

Johnathan stepped forward and started to walk with caution. They came to some tents where people had their back turned to the stream of people. Johnathan eyed a figure with a white suit and thin black hair to the left. He paused and nudged Charlemagne, pointing at their target. The two crept forward to pounce him, and as they stood behind him, Johnathan grabbed him by both arms and tossed him onto the ground.

The man they had tossed, an older, white man with a mustache looked at them with surprise and anger as he was assaulted.

"Damn," Johnathan muttered.

"I'm so sorry," Charlemagne said to them, helping him up.

The man cursed at them in Greek. Johnathan tried to help him, but the man pushed him away before he patted his suit down. He then picked up his hat from the table and walked away.

"Let's split up to cover our tracks and scope out the old city," Charlemagne suggested. "If I don't call you, we'll meet back here in the evening to debrief."

"Roger," Johnathan replied.

The two split up and went their separate ways.

••

Later in the evening, Charlemagne and Mavis regrouped with Johnathan in *Jemma el-Fnaa*. Mavis held the briefcase from earlier. All three of them stopped and sat down at a table in the square. The sun was setting and each of them appeared to be exhausted.

"No sign of him," Johnathan remarked, bringing his elbows to the table and one hand to his sweaty hair.

"We lost him for sure," Charlemagne acknowledged. "Who knows where he or the piece of the Spear of Destiny is now."

"Mr. Cabernet," Mavis remarked, looking at him, "do not feel too bad."

"Oh, I feel upset," Charlemagne said. "To find this missing piece was to be my historical legacy and greatest contribution to the humanities, even if it isn't the true spear that pierced Jesus Christ. The spear is still the one that belonged to Charles Martel and his grandson. It holds a great significance to European history."

"Well, it belongs to Ali al-Suli now," Johnathan sighed. "He's probably back in Dubai by now."

Charlemagne didn't reply and instead took out his smartphone as it vibrated. He looked at the name on the screen, then accepted the call and brought his phone to his ear.

"Charles, it's me," Richard Huxley greeted. "I have some bad news for you that might cut your adventure in the Med short.... You should come home as soon as you can."

Act 1, Scene 2

Diana and Tristan awoke to the rays of the morning sun blessing them through the slits of the blinds around Diana's bedroom. The late-spring sunlight tackled the tanned white skin of Tristan's firm back before peaking over his shoulders and then the paleness of Diana. A morning brightness filled the room and awoke her from her deep sleep of another night.

Diana opened her eyes and felt the radiation of the sun tackle her vulnerable skin. She tensed her body into the body behind her, Tristan, and held onto the hand around her waist. She then looked forward around her room, towards the shelve where her victory ribbons were, an empty carton of cigarettes (the same packet that Tristan had returned to her), the robot head from Russia, her victory ribbon from the Nattau Derby, and a picture of her and Zephyr as well as a picture of her and Tristan in St. Petersburg last winter. On her desk was another picture frame, one of her mother, and before this was Diana's latest read, the Holy Bible.

A gentle breeze could be felt in the room through one of the open windows behind Diana's desk. The light wind travelled inwards and brushed across the top of Diana's dark brown hair and Tristan's strawberry blonde hair. Diana felt the warmth of Tristan relieve her chills.

Tristan smiled as he embraced Diana. He opened his eyes and tightened his grip. Diana thrashed around to turn onto her opposite side so the couple were looking at each other. Tristan opened his eyes and looked at her through her dark blue eyes against his green eyes. Tristan's smile widened as the two looked at each other.

"How long have you been awake?" Diana queried in a gentle voice.

"Not that long," Tristan confided. "Maybe an hour and a half. I'm surprised you've finally awakened."

"Me too," Diana replied. "What time is it?"

Tristan let go of Diana's waist so he could turn on his back and dig under his pillow for his phone. He found it and looked at the time.

"It's almost noon," Tristan answered.

Tristan left his phone beside him and resumed to hugging Diana.

"I like this…" Tristan said to her. "I like that you sleep more when I'm with you."

"I don't like that you're sleeping less than me," Diana replied.

"Well, if I was in my own bed and on my own, I'd sleep my usual amount."

"Well, that's not going to happen," Diana responded, brushing a hand on his cheek.

Tristan laughed at her. Diana pressed herself forward and kissed Tristan before parting. The two then kissed again before breaking off as Tristan playfully rolled atop of her with the covers covering his back like a cape. He held Diana's hands in his as the two laughed at each other with bright smiles.

The couple then froze as a sound from outside Diana's bedroom caught their attention. It was the sound of the garage door opening by the stables. The two of them were looking out to the window behind Diana's desk before looking back at each other with fearful faces.

"Is Charlemagne back?" Tristan questioned, lowering himself and going back onto his side.

"Relax, maybe it's only Mavis coming home from some early morning shopping," Diana suggested.

"Mavis left last night," Tristan corrected, sitting up before crawling forward to leave Diana's bed. "I think it's Charles."

Tristan stood up and walked over in his underwear to Diana's window. He tried to see if he could see anything, but he couldn't. He then walked into the bathroom, past the home gym, and into his room to look out as he saw two figures walking out of the garage. It was Mavis and Charlemagne. Tristan rushed back into Diana's bedroom and grabbed his hoodie from the floor to bring over his torso.

"It's both of them," Tristan warned, picking up his clothing. "Stay here. I'll go to my room and see what's up."

"What's with the fright?" Diana questioned, covering herself with her covers as she sat up. "Charles doesn't bother us in the morning."

"Yeah, but we'll have to greet him back eventually, and I'd rather do it now so he doesn't have a reason to bother us later."

Tristan quickly got dressed in his clothes from yesterday. He then sat next to Diana on her bed as he pulled up his socks. The two briefly kissed before Tristan rushed down to his bedroom. He scrambled around for something to do before he found his laptop and brought it over to him on his bed. Diana entered his bedroom afterwards wearing only her red zip hoodie and a pair of Tristan's grey sweatpants.

"Come back to bed," Diana said in a cute voice, caressing Tristan's cheek with her hand. "It's cold and lonely without you."

Tristan smiled at her and held her hand.

"I'm a little disappointed he's back so soon..." Tristan admitted. "I was hoping we'd have more time to ourselves in the house."

"Me too," Diana agreed, "but whether Charles is here or not shouldn't affect us from spending time alone."

"Right…" Tristan replied.

Tristan's ears twitched as he jerked his head over to his bedroom door. Three blusterous knocks at their door took the both of the them by surprise as Tristan let go of Diana's hand.

"Crap…" Diana reacted, looking at Tristan and then around the room. "Should I go?"

"No, stay," Tristan suggested, looking at her. "It'll be better if you greet him too. Act casual."

Diana looked around the room and then pushed Tristan over to the other side of his bed so that she could sit down next to him.

"Okay…" Diana whispered.

"Sorry," Tristan yelled to Charlemagne, "come in."

The door opened to reveal Charlemagne outside, dressed in his typical suit, but with a flat cap in the same dark grey and material as his suit.

"Good morning, Tristan," Charlemagne greeted, "and Diana."

"Good morning," Tristan replied. "Welcome back! How did your trip go?"

Charlemagne looked at his adopted-children for a moment, looking at Diana's sweatpants.

"You're, uh… back early, aren't you?" Tristan added.

"Yes," Charlemagne agreed, shaking his head. "I know I am. I had quite a trip but had to cut it early due to some unfortunate news I've received from Mr. Huxley."

"Oh, what news?" Tristan asked.

"An old colleague of mine appears to have died recently, and apparently, the funeral is being held later today. I hurried back home as fast as I could. The man was the demolitionist for my old exploration team back in the day, and it appears he had died not too long ago."

"And your trip to Spain?" Tristan queried.

"Oh, forget Spain," Charlemagne sighed with a resentful tone. "It turned to more of an effort than I could keep myself up with. I found myself in Morocco too after being captured by some bandits."

"Oh, I'm sorry to hear that," Tristan reacted.

"Don't be," Charlemagne replied. "But, seeing that you're both up and awake, I'm glad I could vent about all this. I'm also a bit peckish after getting off the jet if you'd like to come down and eat something with me. I would also like if the two of you appeared at the funeral with me – it would mean a lot and I'd greatly appreciate it."

"Definitely," Tristan agreed. "Right, Diana?"

"Yeah," Diana agreed too. "For sure."

"Excellent. Thank you, children," Charlemagne responded.

Charlemagne closed the door and then left them without another word. Tristan watched as the door shut before he turned to Diana. Diana turned to him.

"Charles sound crushed," Diana remarked.

"Yeah, he also looks defeated," Tristan added.

"I've never been to a funeral," Diana pointed out. "My mom didn't have one. My dad certainly didn't have one."

Tristan turned to Diana and didn't reply. He instead took a deep sigh.

"Well, we shouldn't keep him waiting if he's like this. I'm going to grab a shower and get out of these clothes."

"Okay," Diana replied, leaning in to kiss him before she got off the bed.

Act 1, Scene 3

Charlemagne drove his black sedan into downtown Allabrese. The bells of St. Allan's Church could be heard as they made their approach. Charlemagne turned into the parking lot and drove down to find a vacant spot. Diana and Tristan sat in the rear of the car on separate sides of the vehicle. They were both quiet during the car ride. Diana looked out of her window with a fist at her lips. Tristan also looked out of his window during the car ride but was more relaxed. Each of them were dressed in black, with Diana wearing a black dress and Tristan wearing a black suit with a black tie. Diana's hair was straightened, while Tristan's hair was at medium-length.

Once the car was parked, Charlemagne brought the parking gear up and shifted gears. He then turned the keys to turn the engine off. All three of them got out of the car and walked together through the parking lot to the sidewalk. From the sidewalk, they walked down to the steps of the town church. A small crowd of people could be seen outside and lurking around the church foyer as the church doors were open. Everyone was in formal dress and in a somber state.

Diana and Tristan walked behind Charlemagne as he went to the entrance. Next to the front doors was a board that displayed an older man's face with the letters stating, 'Konstantin Nikolayevich Sakharov' above and '1946 – 2018' below.

Diana looked around the crowd of people. The majority of the people around were older men and women talking to each other. The doors to the chapel were closed.

"Wow, this is really depressing," Diana whispered to Tristan as they found themselves in a corner.

"Yeah, I know," Tristan replied, putting his hands in his trouser pockets. "Just keep your chin up, babe. We're here for Charles."

Diana didn't reply but kept close to Tristan. Charlemagne found Richard Huxley amongst the people, standing near Audric Zimmerman. Zimmerman left as soon as Charlemagne approached him. Charlemagne watched him off before nodding to Richard.

"Ralph," Charlemagne greeted, shaking his hand. "Where's Audric gone off too?"

"Oh, he just came to speak to me," Richard replied. "

"Right. Right," Charlemagne said.

"I'm so sorry to have dragged you out of your adventure," Richard admitted. "Was everything okay?"

"Yes, it was alright," Charlemagne replied. "However, al-Suli got away with the relic. I would have had to return home either way because we reached a dead-end. I'll need to continue my search some other time after I do a bit of research as to where al-Suli's taken the piece of the spear."

"Well, you would have hated me if I had kept this from you too," Richard said to Charlemagne. "I know he was your friend."

"Yes, he was," Charlemagne nodded. "It's a shame that he's passed away so soon, but in fairness, he was old and compared to other men in his field, he lived a long life."

"That's right," Richard replied.

Diana and Tristan continued to eye the adults in the room until Diana noticed a beautiful woman enter the lobby. She had fair skin and glistening dark red hair. She also had painted red lips and the appearance of a supermodel in her black dress. Diana looked at her with a frown before looking to Tristan whose eyes were wandering on the ground. Diana then looked back at the woman. She held a designer wallet in her hand and was looking around the crowd before she started to wander around. She eventually started to pass near them.

"Excuse me?" the woman asked in a foreign accent. "You look like Charlemagne's children."

"Yeah, that's us," Tristan replied, looking at her with an anxious face.

"Have you seen my husband? He's a friend of your guardian. You might know him…"

"Don't look any farther," a firm voice said from behind, grabbing her hips. "I'm right here."

The children watched as Zimmerman held his woman before giving her a kiss on the cheek.

"Ah, *lubirea mea*," the woman said, turning to plant her hands on his chest. "There you are. I thought I had lost you."

"No," the man replied before turning to the kids. "Ah, Diana and Tristan," he said. "You both look older than when we last saw each other. How have you been?"

"Fine, sir," Tristan replied, focusing his green eyes on Zimmerman's identical green eyes and looking at him with a slight frown. "Just fine."

"Good," Zimmerman responded. "Say, the funeral is about to start. Why don't you join us and we can sit with Charles?"

"Sure," Diana nodded, following them as the couple linked arms.

• •

At the end of the funeral, Diana and Tristan stood with Charlemagne at the front of the chapel, in front of the open casket. The man had pale skin and near white hair. He also had a neatly trimmed beard and combed moustache. He was dressed in a pinstripe black suit and flowers by his chest. Diana could only look at the man for less than a minute before leaving. Tristan stayed with Charlemagne for about five minutes until Charlemagne finished paying his respects.

Charlemagne joined Zimmerman in the foyer where he shook his hand and gave him a firm hug.

"I'm sorry for your loss, Charles," Zimmerman said to him, patting his back.

"Don't be, my friend," Charlemagne replied. "You have nothing to be sorry for. Nobody does."

"Right," Zimmerman responded, parting from him. "Why don't you come into the library with me for a moment? I have something I need to discuss with you."

Charlemagne looked at him. Without saying anything, Zimmerman started to lead him towards another room. Charlemagne looked to where the kids were and saw them with Zimmerman's wife, sitting on the front step of the church entrance. He then followed Zimmerman into the room, which was a circular library with shelves surrounding the wall except for where there was a fireplace.

Zimmerman closed the door behind Charlemagne before walking over to a table in the middle of the room over a circular carpet. The table had various articles of items atop of it. Audric walked over to it and waited for Charlemagne to join him. Charlemagne walked over with suspicion and hesitance. He had a grim look on his face.

"Are you familiar with the type of work that your friend, Sakharov, found himself in after the breakup of Cabernet Ex?" Audric questioned.

"Well, the crew broke up almost fifteen years ago," Charlemagne explained. "Can you expect me to know what all of us have been up to for the last fifteen years?"

"Fair enough," Zimmerman replied, bringing his hand over to an old book on the table. "According to his wife, he retired soon after Cabernet Ex was abolished, but not before doing some work with Dr. Maxim Ivanov from the University of St. Petersburg. Are you familiar with him?"

"I am," Charlemagne confirmed. "I believe he's an expert in studies having to do with the Near East if I'm correct."

"Yes, that is correct," Zimmerman replied. "Anyways, tragically he died about two weeks ago. Are you also familiar with Dr. Flinders Petrie?"

"Of course, he was a pioneer in Egyptology," Charlemagne answered, pressing a fist onto the table. "He died about a hundred years ago though."

"Well, Petrie left lots behind for future Egyptologists to uncover, including pieces in his own work. According to some leaked information, Dr. Ivanov had plans to go to the Pyramid of Hawara (the same pyramid that Petrie once explored) on his own expedition. The project was commissioned with the help of Tristan Williamson, a powerful English clergyman, who had reason to believe that Petrie had missed a room with some important details about the Pharaoh Amenemhat III and his rule. The notes suggested that Petrie's expedition could not get into the secret room because of complications that forced them to leave."

"Why am I not familiar with this?" Charlemagne questioned. "Why did Petrie believe he missed a room?"

"Well, according to private letters between Petrie and various correspondences that Ivanov looked at, Petrie had located an empty sarcophagus in Hawara, but not because it was looted, but because the sarcophagus found was a decoy. An inscription on the decoy sarcophagus read that only those with the amulet, the amulet of Ra, were permitted to disturb the resting place of the late king and bring him his necklace. Ivanov's notes suggest that the amulet in question was a special one that would instead be placed in a temple in Abydos."

"I see," Charlemagne responded. "So, how did the expedition go?"

"The expedition never took off. It was canceled, alongside a subsequent expedition to the tomb of creation due to various sponsors pulling their funding and political issues that sprung up."

"Typical…"

"Are you familiar with any special amulets in Egyptology?" Audric questioned.

Charlemagne paused for a moment. He straightened up and looked at Zimmerman.

"I'm familiar with one, but its existence is as mythical as King Menes," Charlemagne explained before taking a deep breath and sighing as he looked down at the table.

"Well, with this evidence provided by Ivanov and something else, I think you'll might reconsider," Audric replied. "Sakharov left you something – a journal. He left a note in his will that this journal was to be yours and only yours and entrusted to you. I had a look through it, and I believe it might have the clues you'd need to find this creation tomb."

"For me?" Charlemagne questioned, raising an eyebrow as Zimmerman picked up a book.

"Yes," Audric replied, handing the book to him. "I'm telling you all this and handing this to you personally because by coincidence, there's something you should know. Various explorers and personal collectors have convened in Egypt for an underground race of a lifetime in light of these leaked documents. You are familiar with underground races, are you not?"

"I am."

"Well, this race offers fifty million dollars in return for the Amulet of Ra. An assortment of people have accumulated and convened in Abydos in search of this ancient temple where the amulet could be located, and it's only a matter of time before they do find it."

"And so, you're offering me the chance to participate then," Charlemagne emotionlessly replied, flipping through the journal. "I don't participate in these sorts of things, Audric. I mean, I've just returned from a failed mission in Spain that took me to Morocco, and the danger there alone was… too much. Besides, if Egyptian authorities have caught on to this underground race, they would be on high alert and denying entry visas to anybody with even the remote potential of being a participant in this race. If they heard that Charlemagne de la Cabernet was making his way into Egypt, they would deny me entrance in a heartbeat. I wouldn't even be granted permission into Egyptian airspace aboard the private jet."

"I know money is of no interest to you, and I know about your recent trip to Spain and Morocco from Huxley. I want you to consider this as your duty, Charles, to secure this amulet before these lesser, inferior men do. The Amulet of Ra is a sacred and priceless artefact that shouldn't be in the hands of some collector, but instead placed in a safe and protected location where it can be studied and appreciated by higher men."

"Yes, I suppose so, but still…" Charlemagne said, turning away and sighing. "I'm too old. Cab-Ex – my team, all of it are things from the past. I have only myself and that's it."

"Correction," Audric replied, "Charles, you have two children and that intern from Oxford I recommended to you that helped you on your last trip, Johnathan."

"I wouldn't put my children in harm's way," Charlemagne argued, looking at him. "It's too dangerous."

"No one will get hurt. You'll need them if you'll want to seek entrance into Egypt anyways – entering under the guise of a friendly, family vacation."

Charlemagne brought a hand to his chin and started to stroke it.

"And what about the Pyramid of Hawara? Have people also begun to try and get in there?"

"Yes, but the leaked documents suggest Abydos, not Hawara as the resting place of the amulet. Petrie had his search, missed a room, but what's important is that there was actual mention of the amulet existing. Sakharov left you notes of which will give you an upper-hand in locating the tomb in Abydos. He's entrusted you with this, Charles. You cannot let him down."

Charlemagne nodded and sighed. He held the book in both hands before taking a deep breath.

"I'll have to have a look and think about this, Audric."

"Don't dread too long on the subject, Charles. It is a race after all, and with races there is no sympathy for those that stutter," Audric warned him.

"Of course."

Act 1, Scene 4

Charlemagne exited the library with Zimmerman. The two entered the foyer where an overwhelming majority of the guests had left for the internment. Charlemagne walked over to where Diana and Tristan were with Audric's woman. She stood up from where she was sitting next to Diana and looked over to Zimmerman. Tristan turned around to look at the two of them as they returned. He then stood up.

"We're leaving," Charlemagne said, taking his keys from his suit.

"Yes, we are too," Zimmerman said to his love, looking at her. "We have to get back to Harlech on the double."

"Yes, we can't keep our daughter waiting – she hates when she's apart from us," the woman said in her accent, stepping down the steps of the church.

"Goodbye," Diana said to them as they walked off.

"Farewell, young Diana," the woman said with a smile before linking arms with Zimmerman as they walked away.

"Goodbye," Zimmerman added, waving farewell to them. "Enjoy your summer."

"Bye…" Tristan said in a quiet voice.

"I'll be in touch, Charles," Zimmerman said. "Think hard about the task at hand."

The couple went to a sports car parked along the curb. Charlemagne watched them leave before he looked down at the kids.

"What task?" Tristan questioned, looking up at him.

"I'll explain on the way home," Charlemagne responded in a dried voice. "I suppose we're too late for the lowering of the coffin, so let's just go home."

Tristan turned to Diana and stood up. The two of them walked with Charlemagne back to the car. Diana and Tristan both entered the back of the car and were driven home by Charlemagne. He explained to them what Audric had talked about, and by the time that they arrived at the mansion, he had finished.

"Are you going to go?" Tristan questioned as the car entered the garage.

"I don't know yet, Tristan," Charlemagne said in a strict tone. "I do not know."

"If you do, can we come?" Diana asked.

"I'll think about it," Charlemagne said before opening his car door. "Why don't you two go and relax. All of this is my problem and should be left to me. I'll... I'll be in my study if you need anything. Mavis is around too, but please be easy with her as she's recovering from our last trip."

"Okay," Tristan replied, opening his car door to get out.

Charlemagne went ahead and towards the lift, leaving the kids behind as Tristan went around to open the door for Diana. She was still sitting in the back of the car, cleaning her dress by pulling random debris that managed to tack onto it.

"Why are you so pensive?" Tristan asked her.

"Charles seems sad," Diana answered. "I don't like that there's nothing we can do about it."

"I think he just has a lot on his mind," Tristan explained. "He's probably also really tired from his last trip. He just needs to sleep it off."

Diana looked over to Tristan and smiled. He offered his hand and pulled her out of her seat.

"What do you want to do now?" Tristan asked. "We have an entire day to ourselves."

"I'm going to feed Zephyr," Diana replied. "And then we'll see what we can do."

Diana kissed Tristan on the cheek and then let him close the door while she walked around to go see Zephyr. Tristan watched her before he left.

. .

Charlemagne reached the ground floor and stepped off from the elevator. He then exited the storage closet and walked through the kitchen where pots were steaming over the stove. He walked through the north wing of the house, arrived at the foyer, and from there he went into the library and then his study. He removed his blazer and put it on a coat hanger. He then rolled up his sleeves and went to his desk to check the answering machine. There were no messages for him. Charlemagne loosened his tie and then went over to feed the fish in his aquarium. He looked to the side as he sprinkled the fish food.

Charlemagne's eyes caught the attention of a photo frame resting in front of several almanacs. The photo was from the early-nineties and featured eight smiling faces of the people dressed like explorers from the century prior. Charlemagne looked at the picture and walked over to it. He then brought it into his hands. He held it gently and scanned it with his eyes. He then took a deep breath.

A knock on the door broke Charlemagne's attention. He swung around to look over at the door.

"Oh," Charlemagne reacted. "Please, come in."

The door opened to reveal Mavis entering with both hands clasping a food tray.

"Mr. Cabernet, your lunch," Mavis announced, walking over to leave the food on the desk.

"Thank you, my dear, but you shouldn't be working. Please, take the day off and get some rest," Charlemagne suggested. "You had quite an experience in Morocco and we can survive without you for a day."

"Oh, my trip was nothing," Mavis replied. "It reminded me of that time in India with those monkeys when you were just a little boy," she said, smiling at him.

"My God, you're right," Charlemagne said, giving a light laugh. "It was very similar to what happened in Calcutta."

Charlemagne looked at her before looking back at the picture frame.

"I don't suppose you remember these people," he remarked, turning the picture to her.

"Oh, Mr. Cabernet, how could I forget?" she said, walking over to look at the picture.

"It seems like it was a lifetime ago," Charlemagne said to her. "The old crew."

Charlemagne looked at himself on the furthest left. He had short light blond hair in a combover and no moustache. He was dressed in a light brown jacket with khaki shorts. He held a shovel in one hand and had his foot atop the shoulder as if in a heroic pose. Charlemagne's eyes jumped over the woman next to him with her right arm around his waist and his left arm over her shoulders. She had light brown hair in a French braid and a smile on her face. His eyes went to the next person.

"Kostya died three days ago," Charlemagne said, pointing at him. "His wife said he had died of an unexpected heart failure."

"Such a tragedy…" Maria remarked. "I'm so sorry…"

"Don't be, love," Charlemagne replied. "He was an old, but tough bastard, that Sakharov."

"Yes, he was older than me."

Konstantin Sakharov in the picture, twenty-five years or so younger. He appeared considerably younger in the picture, had a long beard, short brown hair, and was the tallest figure in the picture. Charlemagne eyes went to the character next to him with fair skin and blonde hair, slightly darker than Charlemagne's. He had a chiseled jaw and tired eyes with a fist at his hip.

"Francisco Alonso Cortes Riviera... I haven't heard from him in a long time. He told me he was going to retire to South America and teach applied science. I offered him to come to Harlech, but he refused because of his wife."

Charlemagne's eyes panned to the man next to him. He had oiled black hair and tanned skin. He also had a round face.

"Benito Giuliano Arduino... the rock-headed geologist," Charlemagne muttered before looking at the woman next to him. "Gudrun, our physician."

The woman had wavy blonde hair, glasses and her hands behind her back. She wore a first aid kit at her belt. Charlemagne then looked to the couple next to her. The man in the picture had a muscular figure with long light brown hair in a sweatband. He was dressed in a white tank top with camouflage trousers. He also wore sunglasses over his eyes and had skin similar to Tristan, but slightly darker. He was next to his then fiancée who smiled at the camera. She had dark brown hair in a pony tail.

"Miklos and Tatiana," Charlemagne named. "I didn't see any of these people at the funeral..."

"The funeral was such short notice, Mr. Cabernet. Almost you didn't make it had Mr. Huxley not phoned you."

"Still, Sakharov was family for so many of us. He was a good man. He gave a lot to all of us, and if it weren't for him, none of us would have been able to do what we did or even be alive."

Charlemagne set the picture back and looked at the woman next to him one last time.

"Well, times change and the past is history," Mavis said, nodding. "Eat your soup before it gets cold. I'll go set the kettle to boil and bring you some tea."

"Thank you, love, but please, rest after you do so."

Charlemagne sighed and went over to his desk. He looked at the journal atop and grabbed it. He then walked over to the cabinet next to his desk and crouched down. He opened the doors and began to turn the knob on the safe behind the doors. Inside the safe were several items. At the top shelf, there was a revolver, some ammunition for the said revolver, and a journal over various folders. On the bottom shelf there was a container with various bills in high amounts from different countries as well as his British passport. Charlemagne took the journal out and then closed the safe. He then stood up and sat at his desk. He opened the book and flipped through it.

With a deep sigh, he closed the book and set both books next to each other. He then grabbed the telephone, dialed a number, and waited.

"Hello," a man answered. "Charles?"

"Richard, sorry to interrupt you on your weekend, but I'll be needing another favor..."

Act 2, Scene 1

"Welcome to Egypt," Charlemagne said to Diana and Tristan.

Tristan looked out the window from his seat in the commercial airplane they were in. He could see the Mediterranean Sea where it cut into the land of North Africa in a neat line. Farms fell backwards into the Nile Delta where the patches got aggressively greener. The three of them were seated in business class with their own premium reclining seats. Next to Tristan was Diana, and across the aisle was where Charlemagne was seated. Tristan rested his head back and continued to look outside.

The plane continued its travel and within the hour they were flying over Cairo where the healthy green plains switched to desert. The Nile ripped through the middle of the city and various structures sprouted from the river. On the outskirts of the city were sharp-tipped pyramids atop of a plateau.

"Whoa, they're so close!" Tristan remarked, bringing his head forward to look at them closely before turning to Charlemagne.

"What is?" Charlemagne questioned.

"The pyramids! They're right there! Diana, do you see them?" Tristan said, looking to her.

Tristan looked to Diana who was asleep with her head back and seat reclined. He rolled his eyes at her and then opened the water bottle in the cupholder between them. Tristan then squished his hands over the bottle so that water sprouted out and landed between them. He then laughed as Diana woke up.

"What the hell?" Diana remarked, looking at him. "What was that for?"

"Look," Tristan replied, pointing out the window, "you'll miss the pyramids."

Diana looked out the windows and through her blue eyes, she saw the ancient monuments less than a few kilometers from the ancient metropolitan city.

"What? Is that Cairo?' Diana questioned. "It's nothing like I thought it would be... it's all urban!"

"Yes, that's Cairo," Charlemagne remarked, resting his head back as he relaxed. "Don't worry about that though. We won't spend more than a few days there and instead in the countryside where we'll have to camp."

"Camp?" Diana said with slight worry.

"It'll be fine," Tristan laughed.

The plane began to touch down towards Cairo International. The three of them made their way through customs, and then exited the airport to board a taxi to their hotel.

Charlemagne took his phone out as it vibrated. He looked at it.

"Ah, it's Johnathan," Charlemagne said, reading the text message. "He's asking if I've arrived yet."

Charlemagne then looked at the others seated next to him in the rear of the taxi.

"Johnathan arrived a day earlier to take a look at the pyramids and make some preparations before I arrived."

"Who?" Tristan questioned.

"Johnathan Southern," Charlemagne explained. "The intern I had hired to help me in my mission in Spain. He's a young doctorate student at the University of Oxford, and he came recommended by Audric. He's fluent in Arabic, which was a tremendous help when we were leaving Morocco."

"I wish I knew a second-language," Tristan grimaced. "All I've tried to learn was Russian, but I haven't felt like picking that up again ever since what happened with Yuri-Sergei."

"I know a little bit of Italian..." Diana confessed.

Tristan looked at her.

"You know, just something I picked up around Allabrese."

"Right…" Tristan replied. "Do you know any other languages, Charles?"

"I do," Charlemagne confirmed. "Other than English, I'm fluent in four other languages: Spanish, Italian, French, and German."

The taxi travelled through Cairo and took them to the other side of the river – to Giza. The old black sedan pulled into the driveway of a luxurious hotel where they exited. Charlemagne paid the driver – a local with greyish-black hair and serious attitude. He wore a white dress shirt and brown trousers. He had hairy arms and dark brown eyes as well as brown skin. The taxi drove off after Charlemagne finished paying, and then the three of them walked into their hotel to check-in.

Charlemagne went to the check-in desk while the kids stayed back with their luggage. Diana looked around the lobby of the hotel, which was incredibly elegant with a replica obelisk in the middle. Outside of the hotel were sphinxes by the sides of the steps towards the front entrance. Inside, there was a tall pyramidal chandelier that hung over the center of the marble floor of the hotel. Large rectangular columns divided the room in quadrants with a second-floor surrounding them. The lobby was also decorated in modern beige furniture and fine wooden coffee tables. Various palm trees and ferns were planted in traditional ancient Egyptian pots around the foyer.

Tristan looked to Diana who was dressed in an open-collared shirt with a t-shirt underneath. She wore khaki shorts and sandals similar to Tristan who was dressed in a red polo. The two of them had their school backpacks around their shoulders. Charlemagne was dressed in a beige suit with a white-collared shirt underneath. He also had a matching fedora atop his head.

Diana turned her focus to the fountain on the right-side, which had an ancient Egyptian mural behind it. Tristan tugged at Diana's shirt to get her attention.

"Let's go," Tristan said to her, walking off to follow Charlemagne.

The three of them entered an elevator with staff and their luggage. The elevator ascended upwards to the top of the hotel. Diana looked at the logo of the hotel etched into the elevator floor.

"Tsarina?" Diana questioned. "Isn't that the same hotel-chain as the one we looted in Russia?"

"It is," Charlemagne confirmed. "They're quite a nice chain."

"Let's hope this one doesn't bring us any bad luck with us...." Tristan murmured.

The elevator arrived at the top floor where they were brought to a short foyer. The foyer was similar to the room below but had a table ahead with two pots holding Egyptian star clusters. On the left and right were doors leading into the only two suites on the top floor. Charlemagne went to the door on the right with his card key and swiped. He then opened the door, allowing the hotel staff to drop off their luggage before he tipped them.

Charlemagne closed the door behind them and then grabbed his things. Diana looked around the entrance of their suite. It was a cozy living room with wide windows on the opposite wall, looking down and out to the large oasis lake the hotel was situated on the bank of. Portraits of Egyptian art was hung on the walls, and almost everything was in the same yellow-beige-white color scheme.

The suite had a kitchen on the immediate right-hand corner with a fridge, stove, and sink. Next to this kitchen were a pair of double doors leading into a bedroom. Diana stepped forward to look out the window and see the Pyramids of Giza in the distance. There were shrubs and flora surrounding the lake. She then turned to look around the comfortable couches and loveseats, and the large TV in front of them.

Tristan walked into the bedroom opposite from the kitchen. Diana followed. The two entered a large bedroom with two beds on either side. A curtain hanged from the window on the side looking to the lake and pyramids. A divan was set at the base of each bed, and various chairs and armchairs were propped around. To the left was a door to their bathroom, while the window on the right led to a small balcony. It had a round patio table and two patio chairs. The window was arched and had blinds.

Diana went to the bathroom which had marble flooring, marble counters, and a large shower and bathtub in the right-corner. Tristan brought his luggage into the room, while Charlemagne came with his. Diana stepped out of the bathroom and looked at the two of them.

"Well, looks like the master bedroom on the other side of the suite is yours," Charlemagne said. "You'll need your privacy as a woman, and I believe Tristan and I can share this room to ourselves."

"Oh," Diana responded, hiding the disappointment in her voice, "no. Charles, you don't have to do that – you've got lots of studying and research to do, and you can't keep Tristan up with that. You should have the master bedroom to yourself. I don't mind sharing with Tristan..."

"Are you sure?" Charlemagne responded, looking at the two of them. "I really think you should reconsider."

"No, and if I change my mind, I'll let you know," Diana responded.

"Are you alright with this?" Charlemagne said to Tristan.

Tristan shrugged.

"Alright then," Charlemagne replied, taking his things and leaving.

• •

An hour later, Diana and Tristan walked into Charlemagne's bedroom after unpacking and settling in.

"Is everything alright?" Charlemagne questioned, looking at them from where he was still unpacking.

"Yeah," Diana replied. "What about you? Are you *still* unpacking?"

"Yes, I was distracted earlier when something came to mind regarding the amulet," Charlemagne said, organizing his clothing. "I have lots to do and so little time."

"So, you don't have any clue what's next in this quest for treasure?" Diana responded. "Is there anything we can do to help in the meantime?"

"Expeditions are a dangerous thing. I told you once on the way to the airfield, and I'll say it again: I do not want either of you to get involved, understood? If social services learned that I put the two of you in danger, they'd descend on me and take you out of my care immediately. You'd both be separated and in different homes by the end of the day."

"Wait, so what do we get to do if we're not allowed to tag along?" Tristan questioned, crossing his arms. "I'm not going to sit around while you get to have all the fun."

"Nobody said you'd be sitting around," Charlemagne replied, turning to them. "I said that you wouldn't be involved, but since you're my adopted-children, I have to bring you along and hope that you respect what I am saying when I say to keep your distance. Otherwise, I'll have to pray that you leave the work to myself and Mr. Southern."

"We're not here to be your camouflage from suspicion, Charles," Diana objected. "I'm almost sixteen and so is Tristan. We can handle ourselves. We want to help."

"I already told you my policy for this vacation. I won't repeat myself anymore and just hope you'll comply because you are now aware of the consequences that will affect all of us. I had to restrain myself the same when I was on these sort of adventures with my grandfather-"

"You were half our age then," Tristan argued.

"Enough," Charlemagne said in a calm voice. "My policy is non-negotiable. Anyways, I'm not even sure where this 'tomb' I'm supposed to be looking for could be except that it is in the necropolis known as Abydos. Abydos itself is about a day's drive from Cairo, and I'll require extensive preparation before we venture over there. Johnathan was supposed to prepare for our trip there, but he messaged me saying that he's a bit behind on the preparations. If you want to help, then how about you venture to the *Khan el-Khalili* bazaar and join him?"

"The Khan el-what?" Diana questioned.

"The Cairo market," Charlemagne explained. "I'll give you the money you'll be needing to get there, plus some extra and the amount for the equipment."

Charlemagne walked away from his luggage and opened his messenger bag. He took out two wads of U.S. dollar bills and passed one to her.

"And here is a small allowance for you to enjoy yourselves," Charlemagne added, splitting the second wad into threes. "And lastly, here is some money for you to get around."

Charlemagne gave one-third to both Diana and Tristan before he gave the last third to Tristan.

"Are they going to accept American money?" Diana questioned.

"Oh, I would be surprised if they didn't," Charlemagne replied. "The vendors of our equipment certainly will as they were specific in wanting American dollars. If you want to exchange some of your money for the local currency, feel free to, but beware of scammers."

"I want to get Egyptian money!" Tristan said, turning to Diana. "I still have a couple of Rubles from Russia. I want to collect as much currency as I can from the places we go."

Charlemagne gave a smile before returning to a serious face as he looked at them.

"I have one more clause to my policy," Charlemagne said, looking at Diana. "Given the political circumstances of this country, I'm going to have to insist that you're never without either me, Tristan, or my intern, Johnathan. In other words, Diana, I'm going to have to insist that you're never alone without one of us, anywhere, including in Cairo. Understood?"

"Why?" Diana questioned.

"Because, it is too dangerous for a sixteen-year-old female to be alone in a country like this. In addition, I don't believe I need to say this, but we are visitors in this foreign land, and we must obey their laws as such. I want the two of you to behave and be on your best behavior."

"Yeah, of course," Tristan replied.

"We're visitors," Charlemagne repeated. "When one visits another person's home, we respect and obey their rules lest we disrespect them and dishonor ourselves. Likewise, we wouldn't want them to do the same to us. We would want them to obey and respect our rules and traditions."

"Okay..." Diana replied.

"Good," Charlemagne responded. "Please be back before sunset, and Tristan, if you two decide to eat dinner on your own, please message me so I can make my own arrangements."

"Sure thing."

"And Diana, take care of that camera of yours," Charlemagne said, looking back at her. "You wouldn't want to ruin your early birthday present before your birthday."

"Yeah... I will," Diana replied.

"Good," Charlemagne said, smiling at them. "Otherwise, go and enjoy yourselves while I do some research. Please, don't hesitate to message me should you need anything."

"Thanks, Charles," Tristan said to him before attempting to walk off with Diana.

"Oh, and Tristan," Charlemagne added, "please do keep your phone on vibrate in the least. I will tell Johnathan to meet you two in the bazaar at about three o'clock so that you can deliver the payment. Again, please be careful out there and do not trust strangers. We are not in Canada anymore, and we must be careful."

"Yes, captain," Tristan replied.

"Very well. Have fun," Charlemagne concluded before going back to organize his luggage.

"We will, boss," Diana smiled, taking Tristan's hand and leaving with him. "Come on, Trist. Let's go."

Act 2, Scene 2

Diana and Tristan came to the bottom of the hotel and stepped out to the sidewalk of the city around them. Ahead of them, across the street, was a tall chain-link fence with trees on the other side. Cars passed along the busy road on either direction. The heat in the air was immense. The couple began their journey to the bazaar as they walked down the sidewalk, stopping at a large intersection near a tall condo building.

"What now?" Diana questioned as they stopped at the crosswalk.

A taxi immediately pulled up with a driver bringing the passenger seat window down.

"Hello, hello," the middle-aged local said, waving his hand to them. "Do you need a ride? I give a ride – cheap!"

"Uh, no thanks," Tristan replied, shaking his head before turning away.

Diana continued to look at him as the man insisted.

"Wow, five minutes in and we're already getting molested," Diana said with a sigh. "Do you know how far this Khan market is?"

"One second," Tristan said, glaring down at his phone. "My battery is about to die so I'll need to charge it with this spare battery that you laughed at me for buying."

Diana rolled her eyes as she turned around to shield her eyes from the sun.

"God, how many degrees is it? I really hate this."

"Five minutes in and Diana is already complaining about the weather," Tristan remarked with sarcasm.

Diana frowned at him as he plugged in his phone into the spare battery.

"I'm still in culture shock about Cairo looking like this," Diana said, looking around. "I mean, I guess this is what I'd expect a Middle Eastern city to look like in this day and age, but it's so... bland and commercialized. Oh, but at least there's a Sphinx over there to mix things up."

"Okay, it's about eight kilometers from us, across the Nile, and over... that way," Tristan said, pointing. "We can walk there in about an hour and a half."

"What time is it?"

"Hang on," Tristan replied, "let me change my clock to local time."

Diana looked at him as they stood around with the heat beating down on them.

"Alright, it's just past noon," Tristan stated. "Wow..."

"And what time is it in Allabrese?" Diana questioned, looking at her wrist as if she had a watch.

"Uh, it's about two o'clock in the morning..." Tristan said with a nervous laugh. "That's okay. There's nothing like a late nighttime walk around Egypt, right?"

"We're going to get tired really quick, but okay. Let's just go," Diana remarked. "We can find some sort of caffeine somewhere and maybe something to eat as well. I'm a little hungry..."

The couple turned the corner and started to go down the street. They then started to climb up the sidewalk, uphill, as they arrived at the Cairo University Bridge. The duo then stopped to get a look around from over the Nile to the rest of the city. Tristan took his phone out to take pictures of the scenery, and of him and Diana before they continued across to the small island known as Rhoda Island. From there, they continued until they saw a little restaurant that Diana picked out.

The café that Diana had picked was at the edge of a roundabout after the bridge where they joked about the presence of a well-known American fast-food restaurant nearby. In the restaurant, the two of them enjoyed *hawawshi* and coffee alongside the air conditioning that took them away from the forty-degree Celsius, or one-hundred-four-degree Fahrenheit weather outside.

After eating, the two then continued on their feet along the island, but before stopping outside the Manial Palace to get some pictures. The couple then made their way forward to cross another bridge that brought them from Giza to Cairo. From there, they stuck to major roads as Tristan almost led them down a minor one that Diana strongly cautioned against. Regardless, the two continued on foot and went down the Nile Corniche, which brought them to another roundabout known as Tahir Square.

The square was large and featured a tall flag pole with the Egyptian Arab Republic flag waving with the light, hot wind. Tristan took his phone out from his backpack to get some snapshots before he took some of his photogenic girl. From here, they then crossed the streets to get to the island where three quadrants of grass divided by pathways led to the flag. Tristan recorded their surroundings before he could take a selfie with Diana after failing to grab the attention of people nearby (women mostly) helping them out.

From there, they crossed the roundabout again and began to go around to go down *Talaat Harb*, but before they could get to the end, they forced themselves into a shopping center to see what they could find. The complex was not significant and reminded Diana of underground stores beneath Harlech on the way to the subway. The couple quickly left to get back on their way to the bazaar. They went east into the city and finally found the entrance gate to the famous *Khan el-Khalili.*

The medieval-style gate was not large and went straightforward into the corridor where various people could be seen at the sides and passing along the shops of the market. Diana had begun to notice more people as well as different styles of clothing worn by these people. Some were wearing typical Western clothing, while others wore clothes that went down to their ankles like a long dress or gown. Most of these people were older men, while women wore dresses and head scarves.

Tristan walked with Diana, hand-in-hand, into the market and looked around with disinterest. The items being sold ranged from homeowner trinkets, furniture, and decoration, to clothing for sale.

"So, where are we supposed to meet this guy?" Diana questioned, looking around as they stopped for a moment.

"I don't know," Tristan replied. "Does this place look more like what you imagined Cairo to be?"

"A bit," Diana replied. "I want to find some sort of souvenir to take home… something to put next to that robot head on my shelf. I also promised Moira something."

"I don't know what could possibly beat 'Roberto' as a souvenir," Tristan joked.

"Stop calling it that," Diana scolded, turning to him with a frown. "It's weird."

Tristan laughed before his eyes caught a group of suspicious fair-skinned men nearby, harassing an old man. There were four of them and each wore tactical trousers that were either grey or beige. The trousers had straps around the thigh where it seemed equipment might fit and had patches that the knees where knee pads might wrap around. They wore boots, and two of them wore fingerless tactical glovers over their hands. Over their torso, they wore a dark t-shirt or long-sleeve shirt with the sleeves rolled up over a vest where more gear seemed able to go. Some of them wore bandanas over their head, while others wore baseball caps with sunglasses. The leader of the pack, a man in the center and front of the group with grey eyes and buzz cut blonde hair. He looked young and seemed distinguishable from the rest despite his position. He appeared differently from the others, especially by the insignia on his shoulders. He was also clean-shaven.

Tristan grabbed Diana's forearm to shake her before he pointed the group out as they passed them. Diana looked at them with a frown. One of them in the rear said something in Russian, which caused them to all turn to them. The leader shot his cold eyes at the couple, causing them to look at each other. He said something in Russian to the others which caused them all to laugh.

"Well, if it isn't the children of that rotten old man," the leader said in Russian accent, walking towards them. "I suspect he is here for one reason alone, am I right?"

"Who the hell are you?" Tristan instead said.

"You don't remember us? After all we did for you in Russia?"

"Sorry, we're not familiar with your type," Diana remarked with a bitter tone? "Are you friends of Sergei? Because those are all the faggot-like Russians we're familiar with."

"I should cut that smart tongue out of your mouth, girl," the leader remarked, drawing a knife form his belt. "We lost three good men, and my father lost his best friend, Sergei. All of them in return for that *mudak* guardian of yours, and you two…"

"You might want to back off from them, Kodiak," a Yorkshire-accented voice said from nearby.

All seven characters turned to the appearance of a young man dressed in a scout shirt tucked into brown trousers. He wore a scarf around his neck and had short brown hair that was neatly combed to the shortened side. He also wore long black boots. He looked at the mercenaries with a serious face as they backed off.

"Sorry about them," Johnathan said, turning to the kids. "All of them were raised by wolves and thus don't know how to properly interaction with other people."

Diana and Tristan looked at him without replying.

"Sorry, I'm Johnathan – I work for you guardian, Mr. Cabernet. You can call me, 'Johnny' though. Mr. Cabernet said you had something for me."

"Yeah," Tristan replied, taking off his backpack to get the money. "Here."

"Thanks," Johnathan replied, taking it.

Johnathan put the money into his messenger bag on his side before turning back to them.

"Come on, let's go get those supplies," Johnathan said, walking past them.

Diana and Tristan caught up to him.

"Hey, who were those people just now? How did you know them?" Diana questioned.

"I know them because they're supervisors of this underground race. They're also the ones I had to go through to get us the best equipment we could find."

"But who are they?" Tristan asked.

"They're mercenaries hired by the host of the contest. They're known as the Huntsman from their name, 'Huntsman Legionnaires.' The man you just met was Kodiak Alexandrov, son of the owner, Bogdan Alexandrov. Why were they bothering you?"

"I think they were a little salty with us," Tristan explained. "Apparently, we had a run in with them in Russia last winter, and they suffered because of it. If they're the ones that we ran into in Russia, then I think that means they're the ones that helped Sergei orchestrate the avalanche and blackout. Are you sure we can trust them to help us with equipment?"

"Well, I don't see why not? They're mercenaries – all they care about is whoever has the money. They're practical people, and I doubt they'd jeopardize their status for a little payback."

"If you say so," Tristan replied.

Act 2, Scene 3

Two days later, Charlemagne took Diana and Tristan along with Johnathan Southern, away from Cairo and south into the small town of *El Balyana* on the cusp of the Abydos necropolis. Diana and Tristan rode in the back of a white pickup truck with Charlemagne while Johnathan rode in the front, driving them. They were accompanied by several hired-hands to do some digging. Charlemagne continued to wear lighter colors, wearing a white suit today with a panama hat. Tristan wore a white t-shirt and beige shorts, and Diana wore a hat, white capris, and another open-collar flannel shirt with a tank top underneath. At the advice of Charlemagne, both of them wore desert army boots instead of sandals.

"Abydos is the oldest collective burial site dating back to pre-dynastic times," Charlemagne explained in a loud voice. "Most Egyptologists believe that the king that unified Egypt was buried here."

"Menes?" Tristan questioned.

"Menes never existed," Charlemagne answered. "He's a mere myth. Egyptologists believe that he was a myth to represent one of the first kings, such as Narmer or his son, Hor-Aha. Since their time, many future kings built their burial temples to be with them, and time has buried a lot that still remains undiscovered."

"Well, let's hope we find what you're looking for then," Tristan replied as they made their approach.

The pickup truck turned right at the end of the road where ahead was the Great Temple of Abydos. The truck passed some houses on the right with the necropolis on their left. Johnathan brought the truck to a stop outside of the Temple of Ramses II. He then looked out his window and back to Charlemagne.

"Which way?" Johnathan questioned.

"Good Lord! Look at this crowd!" Charlemagne remarked instead, noticing the wave of people around the burial grounds.

Johnathan looked away from his mentor and towards the group of people in the open desert area.

"Yeah, and they don't look like tourists either," Johnathan said, eyeing them with jealousy. "Where do we go?"

Charlemagne hesitated to answer, scanning his eyes over the field. Charlemagne's arrival had gathered attention as various people within the crowd began to turn and look towards him. Charlemagne climbed out of the truck and walked up to the driver's seat window to look at his intern.

"We will need to split up," Charlemagne explained. "Half of us will go to the true location, while the other one will go to a phony location."

"Which, where?" Johnathan asked.

"You will go to the true location and lead the excavation. With all these people looking at us, they'll only come close and start to dig around me. Take this map and get the others working. I'll take the children and two of the workers to a random area of the desert."

"Yes, sir," Johnathan replied.

Charlemagne handed him a map and then went to the rear of their truck.

"Tristan, grab a shovel. You, and you, follow me," Charlemagne ordered, pointing at two workers at random.

Charlemagne took a briefcase out with them. He then signaled Johnathan to move out once the kids and the workers came out of the truck. The pickup truck rolled out and started to go in the direction of the actual site. Tristan took a deep breath as he felt the morning air and early sun beat down.

The edge of the local village was right next to the Temple of Seti I, or the Great Temple of Abydos, which they had passed. The group could barely see it from where they currently were, two hundred meters away and behind the Temple of Ramses II next to them. Tristan looked at the temple with an unimpressed face. The temple was little more than a foundation with slabs of rock around it and a gate made of three rectangular slabs. The entire antiquity site was in close proximity to the local town.

From where they were, Tristan could see several former sites that had been discovered over time as well as the other people that hoped to uncover a major discovery.

"This place is like a fairground," Tristan remarked. "How long do you think people have been here trying to find the tomb?"

"I would have to guess at least a week," Charlemagne replied. "Can these people not be more discreet? How have Egyptian authorities not cracked down upon this – oh, what am I saying? Corruption is the likely answer to that."

The pickup truck continued to drive towards the cliffs ahead while Charlemagne walked with the kids and workers. Charlemagne looked around for a good location to set up their faux dig site.

"What's the deal with these places anyways? Why did ancient Egyptians do this kind of stuff?" Diana questioned as she tried to catch up to Charlemagne.

"Where else were they supposed to bury their dead?" Charlemagne responded, turning to her briefly as they walked. "Abydos, and others like it, are necropolises. The word 'Necropolis' originating from the Ancient Greek 'Nekro' meaning "dead," and 'Polis' meaning 'city.' Literally, these are cities of the dead."

"I know what 'Necropolis' means," Diana replied, "but why? Why do they do this?"

"It's just a cemetery," Tristan explained to her. "It's not an actual city where people lived. Luxor, the place we were at yesterday, is a place where people used to and still live. This... this is just a graveyard, and all of this is part of their ancient culture and traditions."

"Oh..."

The three of them and the two workers continued across the desert for about a kilometer before they reached a mound where the ground contained pieces of clay shards.

"What's with all the broken pots?" Tristan questioned as they climbed a hill.

"It's ancient litter from sacrificial offerings over the years," Charlemagne answered. "Right now, we're at the site of the very first dynastic tombs dating back five thousand years ago."

The three of them came to the top of the mound where they could see several people poking around several trenches and holes in the ground where pit tombs could be found. The five of them came to a clearing that Charlemagne was satisfied with. He turned around and looked to the others.

"Alright, we shall set up part of our camp here for the time being," Charlemagne said, looking around. "Help me set up the canopy before we start digging."

The workers laid down the duffel bags they were carrying. The kids helped Charlemagne set up the canopy, foldable chairs, and foldable table. Once the tent was set up, Charlemagne sat down and opened his briefcase, which revealed Lucky inside. He turned on the drone and turned it on to fly on its own.

"Right, Lucky," Charlemagne said. "I'm going to have you fly out to Johnathan so we can track the progress of his work. Understood?"

The drone flew up as Charlemagne took out a tablet inside the briefcase. He turned it on and acquired a feed from the drone's camera. The drone flew off and made its way towards where the pickup truck was parked. There, Johnathan was setting up a line for the dig to commence.

After twenty minutes had passed, Charlemagne had the two extra workers leave to go help him out before he let the kids also leave to explore around. Diana and Tristan went to the Temple of Seti I and Temple of Ramses II before they returned to have lunch hours later. Afterwards, they stayed close and laid on a towel against the sand to embrace the sun. Tristan had removed his shirt to try and tan with his sunglasses on. Diana lay near him with her own sunglasses.

"I never thought I'd go on vacation to relax in a cemetery," Diana remarked. "Then again, little more than a year ago, I'd never have thought I'd ever get to go on a vacation."

"I think this is nice," Tristan replied. "It's nice to get out of Allabrese with the right people and go somewhere else."

The couple continued to lay on their backs, looking up to the sky. Charlemagne focused on his tablet as he noticed a group of workers crowding around in a circle. Johnathan noticed and walked towards them. He crouched down to investigate before he rose up again to wave to the drone. He then pointed down to what they had found.

"By Jove, he's found it!" Charlemagne remarked, standing up.

"Huh? Can we go now?" Tristan asked, sitting up and looking over to Charlemagne.

Johnathan had started to order the team to clear around where they had penetrated into the roof of the tomb. Charlemagne flew the drone back and had it hover their current location.

"Lucky, stay with the kids. I'll be back," Charlemagne ordered.

"Huh? We don't need a babysitter," Diana protested, sitting up. "Let us come."

"Stay here," Charlemagne warned before he stood up.

Charlemagne walked off on his own and started to cross the desert to reach the dig site. Diana watched him leave before she stood up and looked down to Tristan.

"To hell with that," Diana remarked to Tristan. "Come on, let's go."

Tristan stood up and the two walked to the edge of the hill they were at. They saw Charlemagne starting his long walk across the necropolis to the cliffs where Johnathan was. Diana waited for another moment before she took Tristan by his hand and dragged him with her down the hill and behind Charlemagne.

The couple walked together and Tristan complied. He turned around as the two walked of and saw two figures that were part of another group nearby come to the top of the hill where they were and look at them. He turned back around to face where he was going to keep up with Diana's pace.

Act 2, Scene 4

Charlemagne arrived at the dig site tucked into an enclave along the cliffs. He immediately gave a relaxed sigh as he felt the shadows of the cliff over him.

"Hello down there!" Charlemagne yelled out.

Johnathan turned around and waved to him.

"We found it!" Johnathan shouted back. "Just like you thought it would be!"

"Of course," Charlemagne replied, coming down the hill and stopping at the edge of the hole.

"We managed to clear out some of the sand to move some of the wood overtop. We might be able to tie a rope and climb down to investigate right away," Johnathan briefed, walking over to him.

"It could be down there," Charlemagne said to Johnathan with a smile. "Could you imagine?"

"It's a possibility."

Diana and Tristan arrived to look down over to where the adults were clearing some space. The drone hovered over them. They carefully made their way down before stopping at the edge where Diana hopped down after Tristan.

"Charles," Tristan said, catching his attention to turn around.

"I thought I told you to stay at the other camp," Charlemagne scolded.

Charlemagne eyed the two strangers at the top of the excavation site. Tristan turned around and looked at them before looking back to Charlemagne.

"They followed us here! I'm sorry!" Tristan reacted.

"No..." Charlemagne replied, squinting at the two figures before giving a warm smile. "It's quite alright."

"Charlemagne de la Cabernet!" one of them said in a deep Castilian accent as he extended his arm out to wave. "*Mi hermano!*"

"Francisco!" Charlemagne shouted. "Is that... it is! Benito, is that you?!"

"Huh?" Tristan questioned, walking over to Charlemagne with Diana. "Who are they?"

"Why, they're old colleagues of mine," Charlemagne explained. "My, what a coincidence to find them here of all places."

Charlemagne walked over and waved to them.

"Come on down, dear chaps!" Charlemagne yelled.

"Nice save," Diana whispered to Tristan.

Charlemagne went over to them as they came to him. He immediately shook their hands as they came into close contact before embracing each of them.

"My, it's been too long, old friends," Charlemagne said, stepping back to look at them. "What brings you to the Land of the Pharaohs?"

"One could only suspect the same as you, Charles," Benito replied.

"My, neither of you have really aged, have you?" Charlemagne sarcastically remarked.

In comparison to how they looked twenty years ago, Francisco Cortes' blonde hair had faded and gone grey. He still wore glasses and had a firm jaw. Benito Arduino had lost his black hair, including his moustache, but retained his oval face

"The same could be said about you, Charles," Benito replied in his Italian accent.

"Come, old friends," Charlemagne laughed. "Come so we can witness another historical moment together. I believe I may have found the Temple of Khnum. The same temple all of these other people are looking for. I can only suspect that you two are among these people in search for the tomb, so come."

Charlemagne led his old colleagues to the pit where they looked at the hole in the ground. Johnathan looked up and over to his mentor as he brought his friends over. Tristan and Diana stood in the corner with the drone hovering above them. The kids observed.

"John," Charlemagne said, "these are the two colleagues I told you about: Francisco Cortes, the engineer, and Benito Arduino, the geologist."

"Nice to meet you," Johnathan said, shaking their hands.

"Ah, how is it to work with old Charlemagne?" Francisco questioned with a hearted tone. "Nice on the first day, and then not so nice on the days after, am I right?"

"Er…" Johnathan hesitated, awkwardly smiling. "The pay and experience are good."

Francisco and Benito laughed.

"Mr. Cabernet," Johnathan said, looking to his mentor, "we've tied a rope at a firm base going all the way down to the ground. I think it would be best if I go down before you do."

"Nonsense," Charlemagne objected, slapping the boy's shoulder, "honestly, Johnathan. You've done tremendous work here, son. How about you take the workers away to the faux site and rest for a couple of minutes? Take the truck too… don't walk. I'll take over from here."

"Are you sure?" Johnathan asked.

"Yes, I'm positive," Charlemagne replied.

"If you say so then," Johnathan responded, nodding. "It was a pleasure to meet you two."

Johnathan walked off and spoke Arabic with the other workers. They followed him in a crowd and went off.

"Such a good kid," Benito said to Charlemagne. "Where did you find him?"

"Oxford," Charlemagne answered. "Although, he came highly recommended from a colleague of mine."

"He is obedient and shows motivation," Francisco said. "He looks strong and determined."

"Yes, and he's been a great help," Charlemagne replied, looking down at the hole. "Now then, shall we get to it? Imagine what waits beneath for us."

"Charles, please, allow me to volunteer to go down first," Benito offered.

"No, that's not necessary," Charlemagne objected again. "I'll be the one to take the risk. You two just wait for my signal, and then each of you come down slowly and carefully."

Charlemagne looked up and around. He then glanced over to Tristan and straightened his back.

"Tristan, could you hand me that torch over there?" Charlemagne requested, pointing to a table near Diana and Tristan.

"Huh?" Tristan questioned, looking at the supplies on the table.

"Flashlight," Diana translated.

Tristan grabbed the two large spotlights and brought them over. He handed one to Charlemagne and held the other. Diana joined him with smaller flashlights that could fit in shirt pockets. Charlemagne turned on the bright light and flashed it down the hole. It provided little light to see anything below. Diana handed him one of the flashlights she had and put the other in the breast pocket of her flannel shirt. Charlemagne turned on the light and deposited it in his own breast pocket. He then grabbed the rope and tugged at it.

"What was it that we used to say when going down dark, possibly endless shafts?" Charlemagne questioned as he got in position to climb down.

"There was always bound to be a bottom," Francisco answered.

"Always," Charlemagne affirmed, dropping in.

Charlemagne carefully lowered himself downwards, inching his way down the rope before his feet touched the sandy ground about ten feet afterwards. He spread his arms out in the darkness, and then looked upwards.

"Clear!" Charlemagne shouted, causing an echo of his voice to shoot off from against the walls.

Charlemagne took out the flashlight and began to shine it around. He had entered a vestibule, or foyer of some kind. It was not a wide room but was tall. Francisco made his descent downwards next with the larger flashlight. Benito then joined them. Diana and Tristan looked down after the third touched the ground.

Very little existed in the room besides the sand on the ground and decorative engravings against the wall. Charlemagne shined the larger light behind him where a large mound of dirt fell through an archway. He then turned around to the opposite end where a large statue of an anthropomorphic man with a ram head was turned over, blocking the entrance into what appeared to be another room.

"Help me move this statue out of the way," Charlemagne requested, walking over.

Diana looked to Tristan before she grabbed the rope.

"Wait, maybe we shouldn't," Tristan protested, putting a hand on her shoulder.

"Or, maybe we should," Diana replied, pulling on the rope before she hopped over the edge.

Tristan rolled his eyes and held the large flashlight in his hand firmly. He then grabbed the rope and went down after Diana. The drone came with them. The two entered the tomb as Charlemagne and the other two finished moving the statue out of the way.

"Whoa… it's cold in here," Diana remarked, looking over to the others.

"Children! I told you to not get involved!" Charlemagne shouted to them in a hushed tone.

"Children?" Francisco questioned. "You have children, Charles?"

"Manon's children?" Benito added.

"Yes, these children are mine," Charlemagne confessed. "They're bright kids, but they were supposed to wait above like *good* kids."

The five of them continued into the next room, which was larger and wider for the same height. Charlemagne looked to his side where he found tall basins with black rocks inside. At either end were larger statues of the ram-figure holding an ax and looking down at them. The main focus on the room was the large mural against the wall immediately in front of them. In the middle of the mural was one last statue of the ram-god, but with his head down. He was human-sized but consisted merely of the torso.

The others had begun to shine their lights around, searching for anything else in the room, but there was little to see or recover.

"Such a pity…" Charlemagne muttered as he shook his head. "I feared it, but it appears that looters beat us once again."

"Looters?" Diana questioned, "but I thought this tomb was undiscovered."

"Looters from ancient times," Charlemagne clarified. "Remember, there's between five-thousand and four-thousand years between us and the construction of this tomb. With that, lots of time before it was buried in the desert."

"There is no amulet," Francisco said in a questioning tone.

"I'm afraid so, like most treasures of the ancient Egyptian era, the amulet might have been looted long ago. I held hope, but alas…"

Charlemagne sighed as he finished speaking. Diana took out her camera and started to take pictures while Tristan investigated the black rocks in the basin. The rocks stained his hand with black markings.

"Is this coal?" Tristan questioned. "If we had lighters, we could probably light a fire for us in these pots. I don't think we'd have too much of a problem with smoke inhalation."

"Here," Diana replied, taking out a lighter from her shorts.

"Uh… why do you have this?" Tristan questioned with a suspicious tone.

"What? Not to smoke of course," Diana argued with a frown. "I brought it in case we'd ever have to light torches or do spelunking."

"Right…" Tristan replied, taking the lighter into his hands.

Tristan went back into the entrance to pick up a bit of wood that Johnathan had broken off from the roof, and he came back to light the tip. He then lit both basins to cause them to light up before he tossed the torch into the corner of the room. The room lit up to give a better visual of the mural.

"Does this mean anything, Charles?" Benito questioned, shining his light on a part of the mural.

"I… I suppose it might," Charlemagne replied with an unsure tone, "but based on the architecture of this tomb and the austere style, I would have to guess that this tomb dates to the fourth dynasty in the earliest. And with that, it means that writing had yet to be invented and so most communications would have been in murals like this one. I suspect all of this to some sort of tale."

"Can you tell what any of this means then?" Benito asked.

Charlemagne shined his light from line to line, going through the entire portrait.

"I suppose…" Charlemagne sighed. "It seems to perhaps be a creation story detailing the beginning of the world with a focus on the Sun. Here," he pointed at a falcon-headed god, "it appears that Ra has sent something down to the Earth – a fireball or meteorite, or something into this centralized body of water. Perhaps the Nile or even the Mediterranean, or even any minor river or oasis around. Here, we have people salvaging from the meteorite and giving the salvage to Khnum, or perhaps, Khnum is blessing them… I do not know what that could be…"

Charlemagne had pointed at a crescent moon design next to Khnum, the ram-headed god.

"It looks like the metal was adapted into jewelry to furnish the elites – nobles and priests, who are decorated with these sort of items. Khnum is watching over them."

Diana looked at the picture of Khnum. He had a fiendish smile and snake-like tongue. She felt goose bumps on her arms, causing her to come closer to Tristan.

"What about the amulet? Could the amulet be one of these necklaces they're wearing?" Francisco questioned.

"Possibly…" Charlemagne simply replied, putting his hand over a cartouche at the end of the tale. "I believe it is best that we document this place and then make our leave. I will send an anonymous notification to Cairo about this site so that they can excavate the rest of it and preserve it."

"I've got photos," Diana pointed out. "If they'll help…"

"Alright then," Charlemagne remarked, looking around for another moment. "I believe then that it's time we leave."

The adults made their way back to the entrance where Francisco led and went up first. He climbed up and was followed by Benito. Charlemagne looked around the tomb foyer as they climbed up.

"Charles," Francisco shouted from above as Benito climbed, "where could such treasure as the amulet be now, Charles?"

"I do not know, old friend," Charlemagne replied, holding onto the rope and pausing.

Charlemagne then looked up again.

"However, based on the architecture, like I said, I would have to say that it is from the fourth dynasty, which gives us a period to work with. The austere style in itself suggests that this was built under Mykerinos' rule and therefore buried with him."

"Excellent," Francisco replied, producing a knife.

"What are you doing?" Charlemagne questioned.

"I'm very sorry, Charles, and to your children as well, but this is nothing personal. I must find that necklace before anyone else," Francisco said as Benito climbed out.

"Stop!"

Francisco cut through the triple braid rope and caused it to collapse down.

"It is a race, after all, so there should be no hard feelings…" Francisco said. "Our client would be disappointed if we helped you instead of him. We are sorry," he added before leaving.

"You backstabbing son of a bitch!" Charlemagne shouted. "What about my children?!

"What a bastard…" Diana remarked, crossing her arms.

"What are we going to do?" Tristan questioned. "They're getting away and know where to look next."

"No, they know of a place to look, but not *thee* place to look," Charlemagne corrected. "Had they allowed me to finish, they would have known. I said Mykerinos, but his tomb has been fully explored with no loose ends. I said fourth dynasty, and although this tomb does have austere style, I believe all of us have made an initial error. The leaked notes that everyone appears to be referencing state 'Temple of Creation,' which was a missing tomb – this tomb, the Temple of Khnum. However, a cartouche on the mural reminded me that like so much in historical studies, there might have been a translation error between similar phrases. You see, there was once a king named after Khnum who ruled during the fourth dynasty, and while I believe this complex to have been built by Mykerinos, he was the grandson of that king who was named Khufu."

"Khufu… but his pyramid has already been explored as well – the Great Pyramid," Tristan replied.

"Aye," Charlemagne affirmed, "but this gives me an excuse to do what I've wanted to do for a long time – explore the Great Pyramid of Giza for myself, because I have always been under the impression that there is more there than mainstream knowledge suggests."

"Okay," Diana responded, looking up to the hole above as she started to cough, "that sounds nice and everything, but we're still stuck down here and it's getting dark outside. Not to mention, there's a fire in the room next door and we can put it out, so we're most likely going to die to smoke inhalation."

"Lucky, go get help!" Charlemagne ordered the drone.

The drone, which was floating over Tristan, floated up and bashed itself against the ceiling of the tomb. Sand sprinkled downwards as the drone lost control and crashed onto the ground.

"Nice…" Diana remarked.

"Stupid drone," Charlemagne muttered. "Oh, we'll just have to wait for Johnathan then. I dread to think about how long that'll take… hopefully he hasn't taken my request for him to take a break too seriously and dozed off."

"Wait, can't we… oh," Tristan said, looking at his cellphone. "We're in the middle of nowhere."

Tristan sat down on the ground, cross-legged, while Diana went over to pick Lucky up. She brought it with her as she sat down next to Tristan. The two then looked over to Charlemagne who had begun pacing around.

"Hello?" a voice said from above.

"Oh, splendid!" Charlemagne remarked, looking upwards. "Hurry! We have to get moving!"

A rope dropped down before Johnathan showed his face.

"What happened? I saw your colleagues leave without you, so I thought I'd come over to talk to you and see what was up. Did you find anything?"

"No. No artefact," Charlemagne remarked to him as he allowed Diana to climb first, "but I did find some clues to where we might look next. I'll explain over dinner, but first, we have to pack up and leave."

Act 3, Scene 1

In the next two days, the family returned with Johnathan back to Cairo and then to their hotel in Giza – the same hotel they had arrived at almost a week ago. Charlemagne had made a call to the Egyptian Ministry of State Antiquities before they left Upper Egypt.

In the afternoon, Charlemagne brought the kids with him to see the Great Pyramids. They rode in a taxi from the hotel. Charlemagne looked out the windows of their cab as they drove along to the necropolis.

"Oh man, we're actually going to get to see the pyramids," Tristan said with a smile. "It'll beat the drag that Abydos turned out to be. I was beginning to think that we were going through this entire trip without seeing them at all."

"I would have taken you to see them at least before we left," Charlemagne responded. "What is a trip to Egypt without seeing the pyramids?"

"The Sphinx!" Diana pointed out as they pulled up outside the gates of the necropolis. "I want to see the Sphinx!"

Diana tugged at Tristan's arm.

"Relax, we'll get to see the Sphinx," Tristan replied, laughing at her.

"Oh, I hope we'll see Francisco and Benito here," Charlemagne remarked as the taxi pulled up to the entrance. "I have to have a word with both of them…"

"Why would they be here? I thought you sent them elsewhere," Diana replied.

"The Pyramid of Mykerinos is the small pyramid over there," Charlemagne said, pointing over to a small pyramid on the left. "We'll be close, but I doubt we will see them."

Charlemagne paid the cab driver and then got out of the taxi. He then looked up and over to the large Great Pyramid before him with his own eyes.

"Ah, it's been too long," he remarked, putting his hands in his pockets before he turned to the kids. "Aren't they magnificent?"

Tristan looked up before closing the car door to step forward. Diana came around to join him. The cab left behind them.

"Wow," Tristan simply said, "they're certainly... great. I didn't expect them to be so big, but they're huge!"

"Well, that's why they're an ancient wonder," Diana replied. "I'm still astonished about how close they are to actual modern human civilization. I mean, imagine living five minutes to these things or seeing them every day you wake up."

"I'm sure they're no different to the locals than the Rocky Mountains are to us," Charlemagne replied. "Come on, let's carry on."

Charlemagne led them down the dirt path on the side of the road. His eyes looked to the large presence of security around the entrance of the tourist site. Security was dressed in white trousers and collared t-shirts. A majority of the security officers were young, but they were intimidating nonetheless with the additional armed private security guards in tactical vests and carrying assault rifles.

"And I thought searching through our bags and the taxi was bad enough," Tristan remarked as they started to step foot on the desert trail to the pyramids. "What's with all the extra security?"

"Terrorism," Charlemagne simply responded. "The presence of mercenaries is to mitigate and prevent religious extremists from getting through to these high-density areas – not to mention, to prevent them from doing any damage to the pyramids. Just last month, the Abu Simbel near Aswan was struck in an attack perpetrated by an unknown terrorist group with connections to an Islamist political group that was banned in Egypt after the revolution seven years ago."

"Oh…" Tristan replied.

"Are we allowed cameras? They didn't confiscate mine when we were at the checkpoint," Diana said to Charlemagne.

"No, your camera is safe," Charlemagne answered. "Just keep the strap around your neck so you don't drop it and so thieves can't grab it out of your hands."

"I won't let anyone touch my camera," Diana said, taking out her camera from her backpack and bringing the strap around her neck.

"At least wait before your birthday before you have something bad happen to that thing," Tristan remarked.

Diana rolled her eyes and stopped where she was, letting Tristan walk forward, turn around to her with a smile. Diana took a picture. She looked back at the picture on-screen before continuing along to show Tristan.

"Yuck," Tristan expressed.

"Oh, shut up, you queen," she replied, retracting her camera from his eyes as they continued forward.

The three of them began to follow a trail that was marked by stalls on the side selling various souvenirs, trinkets, jewelry, and other goods.

"Where are you going?" Tristan questioned as Diana gravitated away from him.

Tristan paused and crossed his arms with a smile as he saw Diana look at the ancient Egyptian themed miniature statues. Charlemagne continued ahead, oblivious to the disappearance of the kids. Diana tried to haggle with the vendor, but he didn't budge. She forked over an American twenty-dollar bill and took the statue in hand before showing to Tristan.

"It's an Anubis," Diana said in a cute voice to him.

Tristan shook his head with a smile before they walked to catch up with Charlemagne at the end. Diana put the statue in her backpack. Some guards on horses passed by behind Charlemagne, catching Diana's eye before she looked over to the Sphinx monument.

"Whoa, it's bigger than I imagined," Diana said.

Tristan looked to the Sphinx as they joined Charlemagne.

"How do we get to the Sphinx?" Diana asked him.

Diana saw gates around the stone walls that surrounded the monument. The walls blocked a full view of the statue.

"I believe if we go down the left side, we can come around the side to view it from a small distance," Charlemagne said, pointing over.

The three of them did just that, coming to the outside of the wall which led into a different, tight structure. Diana and Tristan followed Charlemagne through, turning left and then right to enter a temple of some sort. It had no roof and was merely composed of sandstone slabs stacked up around them. They continued to the left, reaching another doorway that came to an even tighter hall. Wood covered the bottom to provide grip, and the end led them to a point where they could see the famous Great Sphinx of Egypt.

Diana caught a snapshot of the monument with her camera before she caught pictures of the others, plus a selfie on Tristan's phone.

• •

From the Sphinx, the three of them returned to the entrance of the necropolis via the same route they came from. From there, they began to go up a road that would lead them to the pyramids.

It was a steep climb that led to the top of a hill. From atop, they were given a view of Giza and Cairo behind them.

"From the heights of these pyramids, forty centuries look down upon us," Tristan quoted as they looked upwards to the Great Pyramid.

"Yeah," Diana replied.

"Do you know who said that?" Tristan asked.

"What do you mean?" she responded.

"The thing I just said," Tristan clarified. "Who said it?"

"Napoleon," Charlemagne answered instead.

The kids looked to him before Diana looked back at Tristan.

"How the hell are you able to quote Napoleon?" she questioned.

Tristan shrugged before replying, "I heard it in a documentary I watched, I think."

The three of them made their way forward over the sandstone walkway. They passed the satellite pyramid belonging to Queen Henutsen, which resembled a sharp mound of rubble. They then continued onwards to reach the outskirts of the moat. They then continued along until they were able to stand at the closet they were allowed to be near the base of the pyramid. A low fence blocked them all around from going further, although there was a pathway to enter the pyramid.

Diana looked ahead to the slabs, which appeared to be almost her height. From the bottom, she looked all the way up to the very top.

"Welp, I can begin to understand Charles' rationale for there being more to the pyramid than what has met the eye," Diana said.

"Yes, it's quite a structure, but wait until you've been inside," Charlemagne replied.

Diana, Tristan, and Charlemagne continued along the east-side of the pyramid, passing the boat pit. They continued along, coming to the corner where they noticed nearly a thousand people on the other side. About ten times as many people as there were already around them. A lot of them were past the low-level fencing and touching the foundations of the pyramid, taking pictures, and sitting around. Others were sitting as high as seven or eight slabs upwards to have their picture taken.

Diana had her camera out, taking pictures of the structure, the view of Giza from the necropolis, and Tristan. She handed her camera to Charlemagne to take over and take pictures of her and Tristan. The two of them went on to climb up a fair distance to get their pictures taken again before they went down to regroup.

"Where the heck is the entrance?" Diana questioned as they continued along the base.

"Just around here," Charlemagne replied. "Do you see that dent in the structure? That was the original entrance, but the way people go in now is just below it on the right. You see?"

"Oh, there it is," Tristan affirmed, shielding his eyes from the sun with his hand. "I could hardly see It with all these people around."

The trio went towards the entrance and began to climb up towards it. People filtered out it like an ant hill, while very little people were able to get inside. With a bit of patience, Charlemagne managed to let the kids in so they could get to the gates.

"You'll want to put your camera away, Diana," Charlemagne said. "They'll harass us otherwise."

Charlemagne led the kids through the entrance after giving their tickets, and then they began to go through a cavernous entryway that led to a grate in the floor at the side with a set of stairs that went up before turning to a cuboidal shaft that went upwards. The kids followed Charlemagne up the stairs before they turned and started to have to keep their heads down. Charlemagne went up first to guide the kids behind them.

Diana pushed Tristan ahead of her, and so he went first to look up the tight diagonal shaft. The floor was covered in wood with rims to provide grip, and railings on the side. Tristan kept his head down as he started to ascend, while Diana kept her head up to watch Tristan from behind. They ascended upwards until they were out of the tunnel and looked into a larger space that continued upwards.

The stairs split into two sides with the middle simply being a slant above a doorway that went down into an unknown space. The three of the regrouped and Diana looked past the iron bar gate with curiosity.

"Where does that go?" Diana questioned, ignoring the rest of the Grand Gallery.

"To the Queen's Chamber," Charlemagne answered. "There's nothing exciting down there."

The trio chose the right-side to keep along and go upwards. The Grand Gallery had a tall ceiling that was perhaps two-meters tall. Contrary to its name, it was not a gallery as the walls surrounding each staircase were plan and simple slabs. The stairs came together about half-way and continued up in unison for the rest of the climb. Eventually, they came to the top where a simple cubical shaft lay ahead. Grooves existed above it, going upwards to go above and beyond.

"Are we supposed to climb through that?" Diana questioned as they stood around it.

"Yes," Charlemagne said with a smile.

People exited as they waited. Charlemagne dropped to the ground afterwards and led them through. The tunnel was short, less than two feet long, and led into a small gap (the antechamber) that then touched into the King's Chamber. Charlemagne stopped in the middle of the tunnel as he noticed a peculiar detail. It was a grate to the right of the second tunnel, leading into another crawlspace.

"I don't remember this," he muttered to himself, putting his palm over the grate.

Charlemagne quickly dismissed it to hurry forward. The King's Chamber was the main chamber and it was a large rectangular room with the single main and central attraction being the coffin at the opposite end. The coffin was simple in its design, a mere stone box with no lid. The entire room, like the Grand Gallery, had not a single etch or sketch on the walls. Its design was extremely basic and plain.

The three of them went to the coffin where they walked around it, looked inside, and then came back around. Charlemagne looked behind the coffin where a fixture had been placed on the floor. It looked recently placed. Charlemagne then went to the corner of the room, across from the shaft they had entered and crossed his arms. He turned around and looked around with displeasure. The kids remained, while Charlemagne's eyes wandered from the square tunnel they had crawled through and scanned along the behind the coffin where a single cubic stone slab had been inserted into the wall in a position where its removal would not compromise the integrity of the structure. Charlemagne brought a hand to his chin to stroke it before the kids came to him.

"Well, what do you think?" Charlemagne asked them.

"It's alright... the climb was tiresome, but I think this was nice," Diana remarked.

"Yeah, same," Tristan agreed.

"I'll tell you what I think," Charlemagne said. "I think this is one of the worst attractions for its simplicity and fraudulent nature. I intend to prove this when Johnathan and I return tonight. I have reason to believe that the true burial chamber of the great king of this great pyramid was more extravagant than this seclusion room. The authentic chamber where Khufu was buried is elsewhere, and I will find it."

"How?" Tristan asked.

"Oh, just you wait and see, my dear boy," Charlemagne said with a determined smile. "Just wait and see."

Act 3, Scene 2

"Here," Charlemagne said, slapping close to a thousand dollars in Egyptian Pounds into the hands of a security guard.

Charlemagne sat back in his seat as the guard moved to open the north gate for them to drive through. Johnathan lowered his foot onto the pedal and accelerated forward. Charlemagne sat in the passenger seat while Diana and Tristan were in the back.

"I know I said that I didn't want either of you involved," Charlemagne said as they drove forward and down the road, "and I still stand by that statement. However, I'll need your help for this since I'm short-handed. Besides, you won't be accompanying me rather you'll be staying in the van."

"We know," Diana groaned as she looked through the pictures on her camera. "You've told us a million times."

Instead of entering from where they had entered earlier in the day, Johnathan had taken them through the north where an alternative entrance existed. It included a road that went right to the side of the pyramid. Johnathan pulled up and parked the car. He then turned off the engine, and the two of them at the front took off their seatbelts.

Charlemagne and Johnathan were dressed like cat burglars in deep black clothing. Minimal light existed on the pyramid ground at this hour, and the most was the shine that existed up at the four sides of each pyramid. Charlemagne climbed into the rear of the truck to retrieve his duffel bag, while Johnathan followed from behind.

"If you hear sirens... or if you see anything – you let us know," Charlemagne said to the kids. "We'll be in touch on the two-way radio. Do not turn yours off and wait for the beep before you talk."

"Don't worry," Tristan affirmed them. "We'll be here. It's not like we have anywhere else to go."

"Good. We won't be long," Charlemagne replied. "There's food in the cooler if you get peckish and I imagine each of you have things to do to pass the time."

"Aye, captain," Tristan remarked, saluting him before the rear-doors opened.

Charlemagne and Johnathan left the car and started to walk forward towards the pyramid.

"You think they could've parked in a more discreet location?" Tristan remarked as he went to close the doors.

"Yeah, which is why I don't feel comfortable just sitting here for who knows how long," Diana replied, standing up and pushing past Tristan.

"Where are you going? Charles said to stay put," Tristan remarked, turning to her as she opened the rear door again.

"No way," Diana protested. "I'm not an idiot. I'm going to do some exploring. If we're going to get caught, we might as well get caught doing something exhilarating."

"You're insane," Tristan complained to her as she left.

•••

Charlemagne and Johnathan came to the entrance of the pyramid with their bags. The two started to climb up towards the entrance. Johnathan arrived first to a gate at the entrance, which was locked with a padlock. Charlemagne removed a lockpick from his pocket and proceeded to force the lock open.

Meanwhile, Diana had started to make her way forward to the base of the pyramid to climb it. Tristan looked over to her from the van and rolled his eyes. He then grabbed his backpack from the van, closed the door behind him, and hurried over to her.

Charlemagne unlocked the padlock, set it on the ground, and then opened the iron gates. He then picked up his bag and led Johnathan forward through the cavernous entrance. They turned to go up the stairs towards the primary shaft and began to climb.

"Wow, I didn't realize when I was doing my research on the pyramids that the ascent was this long," Johnathan remarked.

"Aye, it is," Charlemagne responded, "and it's my second time making the climb today."

Tristan went over to Diana who had climbed approximately five blocks upwards.

"Where are you going, Diana?!" Tristan shouted to her. "Get down from there – you're going to get caught – we're all going to get caught!"

"I'm exploring," Diana yelled back. "Come on!"

"No, get down!"

Diana shook her head at him as she continued to climb up onto the sixth block.

"I'm going to radio Charles, and he's going to be furious when he learns of what you're doing!"

Diana smiled as she climbed up. She stood up afterwards and unclipped the radio from her belt. She then waved the radio towards him.

"Come and get it!"

"Dammit, Diana! I'm going to kill you!" Tristan replied, stepping forward to go after her. "Oh my God," he whispered. "She's completely forgotten that she's afraid of heights. She's got no idea what she's doing."

Charlemagne and Johnathan continued to climb upwards until they were at the Grand Gallery.

"You see – it's the blandness of this gallery and the final chamber that put me off," Charlemagne expressed as they climbed upwards. "Where is the art? Where is the expression of the king's accomplishments? The glorification of King Khufu? It's all gone. It's missing. It's displaced. It doesn't make sense."

Each of them split up to climb up the steps from opposite ends. They kept their eyes peeled as they looked around to carefully examine the room. At the mid-section, they regrouped to look down together.

"It's all a lie. They were thinking ahead, because they knew that people were robbing tombs that this point. They needed to give the impression to the first to come to this tomb that they were not the first and therefore too late. After all, how could we think less of the same people that built this geometrical wonder?"

"Let's prove your theory then, sir," Johnathan replied, lightly panting. "We're almost there."

Johnathan continued forward up the last half of steps while Diana and Tristan continued to climb up along the exterior surface. Tristan felt a light wind on his face. They were less than a quarter of the distance up, and yet they were still considerably high. Tristan tried to push himself to catch up to Diana. At the moment, they were eight slabs apart.

The others inside the pyramid reached the top of the Grand Gallery where Charlemagne stood and produced a flashlight.

"I noticed an anomaly when I was with the kids," Charlemagne said, shining his light at the grate in the tunnel as he crouched down.

"Curious," Johnathan replied. "Is that supposed to be there? Because I don't think it is."

"Of course not," Charlemagne remarked, "but when I left, I thought about it for a moment until I realized that it might have had something to do with the renovations they had back at the end of the last century. Come."

Charlemagne continued onwards, through the larger tunnel and into the King's Chamber. He then went over to the refurbished ground at the right-side of the casket and slammed his foot into it.

"I believe it might have had something to do with the earlier renovations, but I'm not sure. My memory is not the best from when I last visited, but I do know for sure that no such grate existed. I do, however, recall a grate in *this* room near the casket, which was placed there by the government to cover the hole from when al-Ma'mun and his men sapped the ground."

"Do you think they dug a hole in the antechamber in search for the real tomb?" Johnathan questioned.

"It is one possible assumption. The other could have been related to ventilation. I want to get in there before we start smashing holes everywhere," Charlemagne said, walking away and back towards the antechamber. "I don't think the hole would be big enough for either of us to fit in though."

"If it's not big enough for us, why would the Egyptian government dig it?"

"You assume that they dug it out, and so do I. I do not remember if it was part of the original structure."

Charlemagne came to the tunnel and sat down. He inched himself toward with his legs ahead and started to kick the grate until it broke from its hinges. He then changed positions so that he was on his stomach with a flashlight in-hand. He crawled forward and looked inside the small cavernous chamber before him. It was a dead-end. There was nothing there but a small stone cube. Charlemagne shined his light up and down before turning it off. He then climbed backwards and stood up.

"What did you see?" Johnathan queried, standing up from where he was crouched.

"I saw a wall on the other end, and a stone cube stuck inside," Charlemagne reported, crouching down again.

Charlemagne crawled through and then stood up on the other side. Johnathan followed him. Charlemagne then walked over to the squared slab he saw earlier. He crouched down and placed his palms over the chiseled rock. Charlemagne felt around before he started to slap his palms against the rock. He then knocked on it.

"Pass me the hammer," Charlemagne ordered Johnathan.

"What?" he questioned.

"Pass me the hammer," Charlemagne repeated.

Johnathan went into his duffel bag on the ground and took out a sledgehammer. He then took it to Charlemagne, passing it to him.

"Well, here goes four-thousand years of architecture," Johnathan mulled.

"And a four-thousand-year-old secret," Charlemagne added.

The hammer smashed the center of the square stone, causing chips and shards to come to the floor as it made a large dent.

"Ahah!" Charlemagne proclaimed, raising a finger up as he lowered the hammer. "Did you hear that?"

"I heard… stone smashing," Johnathan replied, reeling from the noise.

"There is something on the other side," Charlemagne corrected, taking a second swing. "The Egyptian government has been so eager to not disrupt tourist activities that they've…"

Whack! Charlemagne made the dent bigger. He winded for another swing.

"… they've not bothered or cared about correcting the history. No, they're satisfied with fiction over truth, and I won't stand for it. I will not."

Diana continued to climb up the ninetieth step or so with a steady pant. Tristan was four steps behind her.

"We're… still not even halfway up," Tristan said to her. "You can still give up."

"Are you encouraging me to give up?" Diana questioned, turning to him.

"No, I'm encouraging you to quiet before you get scared!" Tristan replied.

"I won't get…" Diana stopped herself from completing her sentence as she looked past Tristan and to the city behind him.

Diana's eyes widened and wandered to the side of the pyramid as she felt her hands lighten from their grip.

"Oh, crap," Tristan remarked as he noticed Diana's hand wobbling from where she was frozen.

Tristan hurried himself up the next three towards Diana so he could grab her, pulling her away from the edge of the step she was stood on and into his torso. He embraced her and turned her face away from the city.

"You're reckless," Tristan said to her through her ear. "I still love you."

Tristan continued to hold onto Diana to comfort her until she stopped trembling.

"It's okay," Tristan whispered to her. "You're with me."

"I love you too," Diana muttered, moving her head out to look to him. "I'm sorry."

"Come on, let's finish together," Tristan said to her, taking her hand.

Charlemagne gave the sledgehammer back to Johnathan for him to take a swing, and the two of them had just about reduced the block in the wall into ruble. Southern started to move out chunks into the chamber before he got onto his knees and took his flashlight to take a look inside.

"It looks like we got something ahead," Johnathan remarked. "It's unbelievable."

"I'll let you have the honors then," Charlemagne replied, standing up as he got his flashlight out.

Johnathan crouched down and climbed through, moving rocks out of his path to get to the other side.

"It's another tunnel upwards," Johnathan reported from the other end. "It's steep too. I don't know if we could make it without sliding down."

"Try," Charlemagne simply responding, getting onto his knees to come through.

Charlemagne came to the other side where he saw a shaft similar to the one that had brought them to the gallery going upwards a short distance. The two of them climbed up to the top where another square tunnel led them into another room. Johnathan stopped at the entrance where he slowly paced inwards with his light out to see around. Charlemagne looked at him before he could see for himself what was inside.

The fourth chamber was large and extended forward over the Great Gallery. It included a path in the middle that led forward what appeared to be the authentic resting place of the former king. The walls were detailed with drawings etched into the stone, while exterior to the art were endless treasures.

The path towards (what could be presumed to be King Khufu) contained a drop around it where pillars held the chamber up alongside beams in the ceiling. Charlemagne stepped forward to investigate the jars and vases around with various goods.

"Amazing… it's all still here," Johnathan said, looking around.

"Yes, and it's never been touched," Charlemagne added, standing up as he looked forward to the coffin.

The two of them made their approach to a carved box that lay ahead. The bottom faced them, and the top contained a lid unlike the other. The lid had intricate carvings on it with a sun over the face of the king. Charlemagne turned his attention to the goods around him. There were statues, wooden boxes and chests, and all sorts of golden and silver jewelry. There was also furniture in the form of primitive chairs and tables. In the corner, there was a particular box with no lid with thin metallic chips. The chips were raw and did not have a perfect shape. Its edges were jagged and not flat but bent at random.

Charlemagne walked over and picked up one of the metals and was astonished at how light it was. He looked at it with curiosity, bringing it to his eyes while he held his flashlight in the other hand. He then brought it to his teeth to bite down. It was hard and his teeth didn't leave a scratch on it.

"How bizarre," Charlemagne remarked, putting it back. "I've never seen such a metal before. I thought it might have been tin, or aluminum, but appears stronger than gold or even platinum despite weighing less than them. What have you found?"

"Not the amulet," Johnathan replied, sifting his hand through some jewelry. "There must be tons of necklaces in this room – how are we supposed to know when we find *thee* amulet?"

The couple outside continued their ascent, travelling faster together and coming to the top. At the last step, Tristan stood at the very top and turned the opposite direction to extend both hands to his best friend to bring her up with him. Both of them took a step back to gain equal footing, and then they held hands as they looked around to the ancient city.

"It's one thing that this pyramid is really tall," Diana expressed, "and it's another that it was built on a plateau. I can see for miles from here… it's like being atop of that mountain again."

"Yeah, it's a special view," Tristan replied.

Tristan turned around to look at the stakes that were piled up where the pyramidion was supposed to be. Instead, four sticks were bent towards a central stick in the center to resemble a pyramidal shape. He brought Diana around for them to look at the other pyramids.

"Aren't you going to get a picture?" Tristan questioned as he continued to hold hands with Diana.

"I'm taking this in with my own eyes first," Diana responded.

Tristan brought Diana around to a corner where they could sit down and rest. Neither of them let go of the other. Instead, they sat there and enjoyed the sight of the second pyramid and Pyramid of Mykerinos alongside the high-altitude breeze that hit their face.

"There's nothing here," Charlemagne said as he finished looking through the last vase. "Unless…"

Charlemagne looked to the sarcophagus. He then looked to his intern.

"Buried with it?" Johnathan queried.

"The dead buried with amulets was a usual practice… but it wouldn't fit our clues, but we need to see for ourselves."

The two walked over and took a side each. They laid their hands over the slab.

"Towards me," Charlemagne directed. "Go."

Each of them exerted force and pushed the slab off. It fell towards Charlemagne's feet, requiring him to back off. A musty odor fell upwards at them as they both looked down at the decrepit remains of the former king. Johnathan shined his flashlight down.

The body of the corpse was thin and skeletal. Atop of the bones was a grey charred mesh that extended to the face. The eyes of the mummy were empty and black. The face was oval, and mouth open with all teeth intact.

"He's shorter than I expected," Johnathan remarked.

The mummy was just under five-feet tall. The two of them continued to look at him before they stepped back.

"Well, now what? We've committed vandalism, trespassing, and we're both empty-handed," Johnathan admitted.

"I believe it's time we do what we should have done from the start," Charlemagne replied as motioned Johnathan to help him recover the sarcophagus. "It's time to go to Hawara and find this room that Petrie missed. I need to see the details myself because I cannot work with what Zimmerman has provided us."

Act 3, Scene 3

Charlemagne held a frustrated look upon himself as they drove through the desert farmland of the Faiyum region.

"I don't see any crocodiles," Diana remarked as she looked out the window of their jeep. "There aren't going to be any crocodiles in the pyramid, right?"

"I'm going to let you answer that question yourself," Tristan replied to her.

"No," Charlemagne answered instead. "There are no crocodiles in this part of the country. All of them have been pushed south over time."

"It really takes the name of this region away from being Crocodilopolis," Johnathan said as he drove.

"What's the deal with this pyramid? I could barely find much on it online this morning," Tristan complained.

"Well, there's not much on it for a reason. It's one of the later pyramids that was built as it was built in the twelfth dynasty. Amenemhat III was responsible for this one and another near Dashur (close to Cairo). And there's not much because the inside of the pyramid has gradually become flooded in the last hundred years or so since the last expedition then."

"Some folks at Oxford believe Amenemhat III to be the same pharaoh as in the Bible – not the one from Exodus, but the one in Genesis with Joseph and his brothers," Johnathan stated.

"Yes," Charlemagne replied, "but there has been no concrete evidence to prove this. However, much like most in Egyptologist, there is a shortage of concrete evidence for most of what is believed. And that's it. Most of the so-called knowledge in the subject is just belief. The only evidence brought forward are estimations of time and the curious comparison of Joseph with Sinuhe in the Story of Sinuhe, which appears to mimic Joseph's life to the point of burial, and although it is not exact, the man known as Joseph could have been the inspiration for such character of Sinuhe."

The jeep hit some bumps on the road, causing Charlemagne to pause and hold on.

"Regardless, the idea that Joseph and Amenemhat III could have been in contact is the reason why the canal up north is called *Bahr Yusuf* after it was rebuilt."

The jeep continued to drive along and through the farmland, hugging the side of the *Bahr Salehi*.

"You can start to see the pyramid ahead," Joseph remarked, pointing forward as they made a slight turn.

"Where?" Diana questioned, standing up in her seat as she tried to look for the pyramid.

Tristan stood up in his seat and tried to look around. His eyes hid behind the shade of his sunglasses. He flexed his right cheek as he looked at the pyramid and sat down again.

"It's just as I thought it would look like," Tristan said.

"What do you mean?" Diana questioned, looking down at him. "Where is it?"

Diana jerked her head back around and began to smile. She sat back down again as she laughed.

"That's not a pyramid!"

"Oh, but it used to be," Charlemagne replied, looking at it from afar.

Johnathan drove the jeep along the road to come to a bridge that crossed the artificial canal. He followed a sand path over the makeshift bridge and continued along until he was forced off-road to roll across the free desert. They approached the pyramid from the east and parked the car nearby with all their gear in the trunk.

Each of them hopped off and looked over to the man-made rock.

"Not too many people here," Charlemagne quietly remarked, stepping forward. "I expected there to be more."

The four of them made their approach around the south-side of the pyramid to come to the far-side where the sand stooped downwards. A small group of people could be seen at the simple entrance. It was a simple rectangular tunnel blocked by a simple wooden door of the same size. Two armed-personnel stood guard at the door with assault rifles.

The small group of people were under a canopy, which was next to several tents not too far from the entrance. They had cardboard signs written in Arabic in permanent marker propped in front of their equipment, facing the guards. Most of them were not working, but sitting around, reading, and loitering. One of the party members was an older gentleman with thick grey-white eyebrows and fair tanned skin. He was shouting at the guards from behind a computer. The guards ignored him and stood vigilant.

Charlemagne immediately stopped as he recognized one of the other party members sitting at a desk. She had pale skin and yellow-blonde hair. She looked old – about ten-years older than Charlemagne. She also had a slim figure underneath her khaki shorts and jacket. She wore a pith helmet and had her blonde hair in locks.

"Oh, great...." Charlemagne whispered under his breath as he brought fists to his hips.

The woman looked up from her makeshift desk and sat her pencil down. She then stood up with a friendly smile as she looked over to the fourth of them.

"Charlemagne!" she greeted in a thick Nordic accent.

"Ugh…" Charlemagne groaned to himself as he forged a smile. "Guda!"

"What a pleasant surprise to see you here," she said, coming around her desk to walk over and meet him.

"Yes… both pleasant and a surprise…" Charlemagne responded with a disgruntled tone.

"My, and who is this young lady and two gentlemen with you? Can I assume your children?"

Charlemagne gave a nervous laugh as he shook her hand and then turned to the kids and Johnathan.

"Guda, this young lady is my adopted-daughter, Diana, and the gentleman with her is my adopted-son, Tristan."

"Hello," the woman greeted, shaking their hands.

"And this young lad is my intern, Johnathan Southern from the University of Oxford," Charlemagne added, turning to Johnathan.

"Pleasure to meet you," Johnathan said, shaking her hand.

"Everybody, this is an old colleague of mine, Dr. Gudrun Vidkunsen," Charlemagne introduced. "She used to be our physician on the field."

Charlemagne turned to Gudrun and then looked over to the people she was with.

"Can I assume you are here for the same reason I am?" Charlemagne asked her. "The race for the amulet?"

"Yes, yes," she replied, "but at the moment we are waiting. We set up camp four days ago, but progress has been slow. We hope the Egyptian guardsmen will leave, but they have not. No one is allowed into the pyramid since the race started.

"Johnathan, why don't you take Tristan with you to start the scans," Charlemagne said to him. "I'll remain here with Diana."

"Yes, sir."

"Sorry," Charlemagne went on, turning back to his old friend, "but what do you mean by progress? It doesn't appear that your team is doing much by waiting around, and even if you were allowed inside, the pyramid is flooded to a depth of six meters. Does your leader intend to pump the water out?"

"Oh, no, no," she replied. "Dr. Fischer has something else planned. Come, let me introduce you to him."

Diana followed Charlemagne as the two went with Dr. Vidkunsen to her team's canopy.

"*Doktor, dies ist Charlemagne de la Cabernet,*" Dr. Vidkunsen said to her leader.

"*Charlemagne?*" he replied, straightening up. "*Der Millionar?*"

"*Ja,*" Charlemagne interrupted as the man turned to him.

"*Ich dachte dass er uns helfen konnte,*" Dr. Vidkunsen said.

"*Ja,*" the man replied, turning to her, nodding and waving his finger.

Diana looked at the three of them from behind. Her eyes shot from person to person as they spoke German to the point where she could no longer keep up. She gave a long sigh as she felt the warm wind hit her in the back. She then expressed a bored face.

In the next minute, she stood up with attention as they started to move out of the canopy and go into the desert. She followed from behind.

"What's going on?" Diana asked as she jogged over to catch up with him.

Charlemagne either ignored her or didn't hear her. The four of them intersected with Tristan and Johnathan as they were carrying some measuring tape and other interesting equipment. Charlemagne stopped at them and quickly introduced Dr. Fischer to the two of them.

"Put that equipment back," Charlemagne ordered them. "We're going to join up with this team since they've already done their scans and found a possible alternate entrance."

"Okay..." Johnathan replied as they walked off.

Tristan eyed Diana, and the two looked at each other briefly before they were torn apart again. Charlemagne walked with Dr. Fischer and Dr. Vidkunsen to the edge of the canal where diggers were working under the supervision of a man younger than Dr. Fischer, but who appeared to be Turkish. He wore a dark tanned collared shirt similar to what Tristan was wearing but had deep sweat stains and had his shirt unbuttoned to reveal his chest hair and torso.

Dr. Fischer introduced the man (Hossan) to Charlemagne before they looked towards a tunnel where three workers were digging in. It was mildly deep and slanted, going into the earth for at least five meters.

"*Wir haben gerade das Dach gefunden,*" Dr. Fischer explained to Charlemagne.

The adults continued to chat to one another in a language that Diana could not understand. Diana sighed and brought her hand to her neck to shield it from the sun. Johnathan and Tristan later re-appeared to join them. Charlemagne broke off from the others and went to the boy and the intern with Diana.

"What's going on?" Johnathan questioned.

"According to Dr. Fischer, his team has discovered the supposed Labyrinth of Herodotus underneath our very feet. I've reviewed his work and am a little a skeptical of his findings. It's a stretch but could be what Dr. Petrie was talking about when he mentioned he had 'unfinished work.'"

"Charles..." Johnathan said, lowering his voice, "can we trust this man? They're not working with us from the bottom of their heart – they want something from us – our help."

"Indeed, I understand your concern," Charlemagne replied, turning to face them, "but don't worry, son. I am equally suspicious of them, especially after we... rather, I was backstabbed by my other old colleagues. Rest assured, I know what I am doing..."

"*Nun, Herr Cabernet?*" Dr. Fischer questioned, walking over towards them.

Charlemagne went over to him. The others followed from behind and came over.

"Johnny, you speak German," Tristan said to him as they stood behind Charlemagne. "What are they saying?"

"Uh... I don't speak it so much as I can understand and read it," Johnathan corrected, "but they're talking about going in... however they're not sure if there is going to be water in the tunnels. Apparently they want Charlemagne to help them translate whatever they find since he's good at it."

The group turned to the tunnel as Hossan shouted in German.

"*Ah, gut!*" Dr. Fischer said, leading them towards the tunnel as workers vacated.

Charlemagne walked forward to join him into the tunnel, but stopped at the entrance with Dr. Vidkunsen, the kids, and Johnathan. He turned to the kids as the doctor went into the tunnel.

"Dr. Fischer has asked me to go into the tunnel on my own," Charlemagne said to them before leading them away from the tunnel. "I do not trust him, especially now that he's said that he intends to send a drone with us to substitute him because of supposed 'arthritis' issues. I asked what off you kids, and Gudrun has said that she would look after you..."

"Hell no," Tristan replied.

"I know," Charlemagne said, raising a palm for Tristan to be quiet and calm down. "It is not that I do not think well of Gudrun

– she's saved my life a many of times – but we are on opposing sides this time, which is why I am asking you two to come with me. It will be dangerous, and so I need you to realize that and be on your best behavior."

"Of course," Diana replied.

"Yeah," Tristan added.

"What about me?" Johnathan asked.

"You will need to stay here as our insurance policy. I want you to stay close to them, brief me on anything important that they might be saying to one another, or of anything suspicious. We will be on a private channel on our own two-way radios. It'll be good practice for you to work on your German, my dear boy. There are a lot of Germans active in Egyptology," Charlemagne said, smiling at him as he patted him on the shoulder. "You are also armed, so don't let them intimidate you. Besides, you have Egyptian authorities close by, so I expect little of their funny games on us. Please, don't try to endanger yourself at the same time."

"*Herr Cabernet?*" Dr. Fischer called from the tunnel.

Charlemagne turned to face the tunnel.

"*Ja?*" he questioned.

Charlemagne didn't get a response so he went over to the tunnel, leaving the kids outside as he passed Dr. Vidkunsen. He stopped her for a moment.

"Please help the children get ready, will you, old friend?" Charlemagne asked her. "They've insisted to come with me, and I simply cannot say no to them."

"Oh, that's alright, Charles," Gudrun replied. "I will help them out."

"Thank you."

Dr. Vidkunsen came out of the tunnel and looked at the kids. She then left for a brief moment before returning with the workers who carried various equipment with them. The two of them were given headlamps to wear across their foreheads. Dr. Vidkunsen also entrusted a first aid kit to Diana, and then gave them their safety harnesses for their descent into the tunnel.

Tristan took off his backpack and Dr. Vidkunsen took it from him so that he could put on his harness. Diana did the same afterwards since she had to hold the first aid kit momentarily and became lost as she looked at Tristan getting ready. She handed him the first aid kit to him so that she could take off her backpack and give it to Dr. Vidkunsen. She put on her harness and then received her backpack again as Charlemagne came out of the tunnel.

Charlemagne watched as Diana's backpack was exchanged before being approached from the side by a worker with gear. Charlemagne readied himself up with his own first aid kit, harness, and headlamp. He then went back down into the tunnel with Hossan and the kids.

Hossan laid out a steel-wire tether behind him and allowed Charlemagne to go first. A worker came down behind them, carrying a small drone – a miniature unmanned-ground vehicle with tracks at the side and a camera in the middle with an antenna sticking out from the rear. The worker put the drone into Hossan's arms as Charlemagne started to lower himself. He gently made the climb downwards, reaching the bottom of the tunnel below with his own feet. The drop was about two meters.

Charlemagne looked around from side to side as he could see two directions for him. A bit of sand descended downwards and fell over him as he looked up. He coughed before stepping out of the way.

"*Klar!*" he shouted.

Act 3, Scene 4

After the kids lowered themselves into the maze, the drone was gently brought down and activated. It took about fifteen minutes to make sure the others could receive a signal through the earth, which gave Charlemagne ample time to have Tristan secure a radio channel so they could likewise be in contact with Johnathan on the surface. Charlemagne held the two-way radio given to him by Dr. Fischer while Tristan carried the one for communication with Johnathan.

"Alright, now what?" Charlemagne muttered to himself as he stood up and looked around.

Charlemagne took a deep breath as he looked around the tunnel. He brought the palm of his hand to the plain wall to his right, and then he looked to the similar plan wall on the left. The floor and roof were chiseled stone with no unique markings, writings, or art on the walls. Tristan looked up at the hole they had come through where the only source of light – a ray of light seeped from above.

In either direction before them, absolute darkness followed.

"Well, what direction now?" Tristan asked, feeling a chill against his warmed skin.

"I don't know," Charlemagne replied, "producing a journal from within his jacket. According to notes left behind by my old friend, this labyrinth is supposed to connect to a central hidden chamber, which then leads to the true burial chamber discovered briefly by Petrie. He left behind instructions for opening some sort of a hidden door, but there is little here about the actual tomb. I have some references to some earlier scholars who had tried to map the maze, but the validity and accuracy is questionable by my standards."

Some static began to transmit from the radio clipped to Charlemagne's belt. Charlemagne picked up the radio and brought it close to him. He altered the volume as static continued to filter through.

"Charles... this is Guda," Dr. Vidkunsen said in English.

"Hello, doctor," Charlemagne replied, putting his book away.

"Dr. Fischer is examining his maps in relation to your location," the doctor explained. "We will start to move the drone when we are confident in where you need to go. Just follow it."

"I would assume we should start to walk in the direction towards the pyramid," Charlemagne replied, closing his eyes for a moment before opening them. "The edge of the labyrinth was said to be over the *Bahr Saleh* so I assume that we are somewhere in the middle perhaps?"

No response came from the radio.

"Couldn't they have figured a path beforehand? You know, while they were just sitting around doing nothing," Tristan complained, leaning against a wall.

Diana stood close to Tristan in the cold tunnel. Charlemagne ignored Tristan and continued to look at either directions. Diana jerked her head to the right as she heard some painful moaning come from the distance. Her eyes widened and breathing picked up. She grabbed Tristan's hand tightly.

"Did you hear that?" Diana asked with fixed eyes ahead.

"Hear what?" Tristan questioned, looking at him.

"That noise."

"What noise?"

"N-never mind," Diana replied, swallowing her breath before looking back to him. "It was probably just some wind, or something. I don't know."

"Hello?" Charlemagne called into the radio.

Again, there was no response.

"Tristan, give me your radio," Charlemagne ordered, putting his back onto his belt clip.

Tristan gave him the radio.

"Johnathan, what is going on?" Charlemagne asked.

Charlemagne let go of the microphone and waited for a response.

"Johnathan, come in…" Charlemagne asked again.

"Great…" Tristan remarked, looking at Charlemagne, "they've trapped us down here, haven't they?"

"Hello? Hello?" Johnathan responded to Charlemagne. "Mr. Cabernet – what's going?"

"What's going on, is that Dr. Fischer and his colleagues have gone dark on us, and we have no idea which direction we ought to go," Charlemagne explained with fury. "What are they doing?"

Some static picked up in response to Charlemagne alongside some muffled, but mostly inaudible words from Johnathan.

"Say again?" Charlemagne asked. "The reception is bad."

"Dr. Fischer is looking at a map," Johnathan said again with static in the background. "He's not sure where you are in relation to the maze… Oh… Hang on… I think they're about to move the drone."

Charlemagne turned around and looked at the drone. Its camera rotated around before it began to make its way towards Charlemagne and then went around. It started to go east.

"Well, it's something. Come on, let's not get lost," Charlemagne said.

"You know, I think this might actually be a bad idea," Diana remarked as they let Charlemagne and the drone lead.

"Don't worry, we'll be fine," Tristan remarked, holding onto Diana's hand as they went forward.

"I'm having a hard time believing you…"

Within the first several yards, Charlemagne noticed an option to turn left into a short tunnel that turned soon again. The drone ignored this option and continued forward instead. They soon passed another, similar option before coming towards a small vestibule. The robot stopped here and turned to the right. Charlemagne looked and saw a large entrance that led south into another rectangular room, which was completely empty.

Charlemagne looked down at the drone and through about where they were.

"What's going on…" Charlemagne muttered to himself with worry.

The drone turned its camera away from the room and continued forward. It then stopped at the first intersection with a short tunnel going left. Some static picked up from the other radio. Charlemagne passed his radio back to Tristan and took the other.

"Dr. Fischer asks that you wait here," Dr. Vidkunsen said over the static.

Charlemagne did not respond and watched as the drone went forward. It then turned and disappeared.

"Dammit, I knew I should have done my own sonar scans," Charlemagne said, turning to the kids. "I'm sorry about this."

"Stop apologizing, Charles," Tristan said. "We know what we signed up for."

"Well, partially," Diana remarked, letting go of Tristan's hand to stretch her arms up.

"It seems like these off-chutes run all along this wall," Charlemagne said, looking ahead. "I have no doubt that some of them might be dead-ends or serve to confuse anybody's sense of direction."

"Come through," Dr. Vidkunsen said, cutting Charlemagne off. "It is clear."

"Understood," Charlemagne responded to the radio before looking to the kids. "Come on."

Charlemagne led them down the short tunnel, which turned both left and right. Charlemagne followed the path of the drone and went left and then down before going right and then up. He found the drone in a three-way intersection ahead, with new options left and right. They met up with it and looked.

"Oh great, another layer," Diana said, grabbing Tristan's hand again as he looked around.

"Yes, it appears to be another layer," Charlemagne agreed, looking both ways.

The drone led them down the right and then stopped at a larger intersection with a larger hallway going north. The north hall was much wider and had pillars on the side. Charlemagne shined his light down and could see doors in the left and right ahead along with another wide intersection ahead. The robot made the option to keep going ahead and so Charlemagne followed it with the kids behind him.

The group passed about five intersections before coming against another three-way intersection like the opposite side. The drone made the immediate option to the right and then left to go down another narrow tunnel that led into an area similar to where they had arrived. The robot then turned left and came into another vestibule. It then went into the larger room and stopped.

Charlemagne looked around this room before stretching his hand over to Tristan to take the radio. Tristan gave it to him.

"Johnathan, I believe we are close to you. I also believe we are at the medial base of the pyramid on the south side, but it appears that we've hit a dead-end."

"Yeah, I'm following along," Johnathan replied.

"Doctor, what is going on?" Charlemagne asked, switching radios.

No response came. Instead, the drone left the room and turned left. It continued down the hall before coming to another dead-end.

"Charles... north-most side..." Dr. Vidkunsen said over the radio.

"I'm sorry? Say again?" Charlemagne requested.

"Charles, you are on the north-most side of the maze. Dr. Fischer has asked that you search for any possible irregularities or possible entrances into the pyramid from where you are."

"Understood," Charlemagne replied. "I'll see what I can find."

Charlemagne clipped the radio back onto his belt and gave the other to Tristan. He looked around the plain corridor. He then turned to the kids, which prompted them to part hands.

"They are above us and the entrance to the pyramid is above us by at least five or seven meters. For some reason, this maze is not flooded, which tells me that wherever this connection is, it is sealed tight and cut-off from the water leaking in from the river. Come with me..."

Charlemagne led the kids down and back into the vestibule. He then turned left in the squared room to look around. He stood in the middle while the kids hung at the door frame. Tristan watched Charlemagne with focused eyes. Charlemagne opened his arms and stepped forward. He hugged the wall and began to feel around.

"What the hell is he doing?" Diana questioned in a soft tone.

"Shush," Tristan replied.

Charlemagne carefully examined the wall, dragging his fingernails over the stone before he felt an extremely tiny slit.

"Ahah!"

"What is it?" Tristan asked.

Charlemagne followed the slit with his nail and saw that it went all the way down to the ground. He then stood up again and followed it upwards. He came to the left-side of the far wall and tried to find a similar slit. Once he found it, he came to the middle and pushed his palms against the wall.

"No, that never works," Charlemagne remarked, stepping back before turning to the kids. "I believe I've found a hidden door. No water seems to be seeping through, but I do not think it's because of the tightness around this entrance. All of this would have been flooded regardless if there were water on the other side."

"How do we get through?" Tristan asked.

"I'm working on that, but my guess would be some sort of pressure panel on the wall. Help me out and hug the wall for me. Feel for anything odd," Charlemagne requested, going back to the door to hug it himself.

Diana looked at Tristan with uncertainty before they split to take a side of the wall. Nobody found anything.

"I should have packed a sledgehammer, or a pickaxe with us before we went down," Charlemagne said, placing a palm against the wall as he looked over to the kids.

Diana and Tristan looked back at him before they looked over to the entrance they had come through. The drone had arrived and found them.

"Great, and I don't suppose you've found anything," Charlemagne mocked at the primitive robot as he pressed against the wall.

"What if we pushed against the door with all our force?" Tristan offered. "We might be able to move it manually."

"Yes, I suppose that's our Plan B," Charlemagne replied, standing up and going to the wall.

All three of them positioned themselves and pressed their hands against the door. Each of them planted their feet onto the stone ground.

"On my mark…" Charlemagne said. "Push!"

The three of them pushed against the wall, causing the stone to budge. Charlemagne broke off and looked at the wall with a smile.

"Ah, you see! It moves…" he said, panting. "Once more!"

The three pushed again on his mark, and the stone moved again, sliding open on an axis that ran on the middle of the stone. It moved only ninety-degrees before stopping.

"Well done, Charles," Dr. Vidkunsen said over the radio.

"Yes…" Charlemagne replied without picking up the radio, still panting. "Come on."

Charlemagne led onwards into the tunnel and they came down a large and wide corridor to reach a larger squared room with pillars in a square, one or two meters from the outer perimeter. Charlemagne came to the pillars and looked in the middle where a single tomb casket stood with a large pit above that, which went into darkness. Diana and Tristan joined up.

Tristan noticed tunnels on the left and right from where they went, so he pointed them out to Charlemagne who went over to investigate.

The tunnel went down and into a pool of water below. Charlemagne returned and stepped into the central space which was on a lower-level than the surrounding. It also contained a shallow bit of water. He came to the casket and looked at the top. There were no engravings or words written. He then looked up and looked around to the pillars and walls. There were no markings on those either.

"Well, this doesn't seem right…" Charlemagne said, turning to the drone.

The drone was paused underneath the door from between the current room and earlier corridor. It looked at Charlemagne, which caused him to pick up his radio and hold down to transmit.

"What does Dr. Fischer make of this, doctor?" he questioned.

Charlemagne's voice echoed in the chamber, but no response came through.

"Doctor?" Charlemagne questioned again.

Charlemagne rolled his eyes and went over to the robot. He squatted down and waved his hand over the camera. He then checked to see if it was on, or if the battery had died, but it hadn't and it was on. He then looked to the side of the drone to see a red light near the antenna. The light was blinking.

"Great..." Charlemagne muttered, standing up and going back to the casket. "Children, come along here and help me open this. It could be that this tomb was looted long ago, so we might as well check the mummy to confirm if the casket is empty or not."

The kids came over and each took a side next to Charlemagne. They brought their hands to the side of the lid and on Charlemagne's mark, they pushed it open. It took a bit of force, but not as much as it took them earlier to open the hidden door. The stone fell over, causing a whirl of pressurized air to escape from within.

"Oh God! What is that stench?!" Tristan remarked, stepping back and plugging his nose.

"It smells like... something fermenting..." Diana replied, frowning.

Charlemagne flared his nostrils to catch the scent, but instead he focused on what was inside. There was no mummy – instead, there was more.

"My God," Charlemagne remarked, "it goes deeper."

Charlemagne looked down into the casket to see that it was in fact an entrance into the tomb below. He took out Sakharov's journal and flipped to the notes.

"Of course," Charlemagne said, "we were just at the hidden entrance, which means... those tunnels over there lead out. The flooding has caused the air tunnels of this faux tomb to become easily passable for us."

Charlemagne wrote something before putting the book away. He then unlatched his own backpack and began to take some rope out. He went to one of the pillars to tie the rope around and then went to the entrance to drop the other end below.

"Wait here," Charlemagne ordered, "I'm going down. Do not follow me this time. You have come far enough. Stay here, please."

"Alright," Diana replied, watching him enter and descend, "such a party pooper."

Charlemagne lowered himself down about ten yards below until he touched solid ground near the genuine casket. This sarcophagus had writing and artwork over top.

"Amenemhat..." Charlemagne whispered, looking at the coffin before turning around.

Charlemagne shined his light at all the treasure around where glistening gold and polished wooden furniture embellished the room and almost hid the wall around. Artwork decorated around with words overtop. He spun around the room and immediately opened his backpack to take out lamps to further brighten the chamber.

"Johnathan, do you read me?" Charlemagne asked.

No response came. Charlemagne instead started to document the room as he took pictures of every wall and then the sarcophagus. He put a palm over the inscriptions over the lid and scurried into his backpack to take thin sheets of paper to lay overtop. He then produced a piece of granite to trace the words.

Once he was finished, in his excitement, he traced his eyes over the words.

"My God, Petrie was right...! Sakharov was right! They were all right! The amulet does exist!"

"How's it going down there, Charles," Tristan questioned, looking down.

"More than perfect, my dear boy!" Charlemagne exclaimed. "It exists! The amulet actually exists! 'A special amulet constructed for his royal highness, King Amenemhat III, to be worn by all his successors hence forth.' Oh, we were wrong to be looking where we were looking!"

Charlemagne's eyes continued to trace the paper.

"Where- ah, yes! Here, 'An amulet to be guarded in the Temple of Creation, facing its sister in... Karnak.' Karnak? What sister? Another amulet?"

Tristan looked to Diana with a smile.

"I'm glad we're making progress," Tristan said to her.

"Okay, I'm glad, but while you're feeling happy for him, I'm starting to question how the hell we're going to get out of here," Diana said, eyeing around. "Do you think others will help us in exchange for this information?"

"As long as they don't think we've backstabbed them by sabotaging the drone," Tristan said.

"You sabotaged the drone?" Diana questioned with alert.

"No, did you?" Tristan asked.

"No."

Charlemagne continued to examine the rest of the casket's inscriptions. He then looked up to see what was a large depiction of two circles. Charlemagne squinted at them before looking at two deity figures at either side. There were some words above.

He took his camera out and went over to take a picture before reading it.

"Disks…" Charlemagne muttered, "of the Great Fireball."

Charlemagne produced his own journal from his jacket and began to flip through it. He then read out something he had written.

"It can't be," Charlemagne muttered. "The same orbs? Mantuhotep? The meteorite? The metals? My God."

Charlemagne's smile had faded and been replaced with fear. He put his journal away in his backpack and produced Sakharov's journal to put it in his backpack as well. He then went over to the treasure, taking out a bottle of kerosene and hatchet. He then went to some barrels and swung the hatchet against the lids, causing red liquid to pour out. He did this to every barrel he could find, causing the smell of wine to take over the rotten smell of the chamber. With the bottle of kerosene, he began to pour it anywhere that the alcohol didn't meet, including over the wooden sarcophagus of the king.

Once he was done, he put the bottle and hatchet away, and grabbed the rope. Charlemagne climbed up and out of the tomb. Tristan helped him out once he could, helping him climb out. Charlemagne fell to his knees after falling over and immediately stood up to look at the kids.

"What did you find? Any sign of the amulet? Any new leads?"

"A lead? Yes. The amulet? No. Amenemhat was not buried nor meant to be buried with the amulet. I'll explain later because we need to leave."

"*Hallo?*" a deep voice echoed down the hall? "Herr Cabernet?"

"Let's go," Charlemagne said, holding his gas lamp in hand before turning to the pit.

"What are you doing?" Tristan questioned, watching him hover the lamp over the hole.

Charlemagne dropped the lamp into the tomb.

"Let's go!" Charlemagne shouted, grabbing and pushing each of them to go forward.

The trio ran towards one of the two tunnels.

"What the hell?!" Tristan questioned, turning around as an eruption of fire came out of the tomb hole.

The ground beneath them shook, which gave Tristan motivation to continue going forward. The three of them reached the tunnel and Charlemagne hurried into the water, trudging through.

"Crap… we're going to have to swim?!" Diana questioned, stopping Tristan at the edge of the water.

Charlemagne, who was already waist-deep in the water, turned around and looked at Diana with alert.

"Oh, damn! I forgot that you can't swim."

"She can swim," Tristan countered, looking at Charles. "I taught her. She's just not very good at it…"

Diana frowned at him.

"Hold my hand, or better yet, put your hands around my waist," Tristan said to her. "I'll lead us. Let's just…"

Another explosion set off in the tomb. Tristan's didn't finish his words, instead, Diana quickly wrapped her arms around his waist and Tristan hurried into the water. For a brief moment, the head lamps around their foreheads lit the way for them before flickering and dying out. Charlemagne took the lead and led Tristan down the narrow tube before they came into a small chamber. From here, they went into a horizontal tunnel that then led upwards and out.

Charlemagne ran out of the water once he could after submerging. He then turned around to help Tristan with Diana on his back, pulling them out of the water as they coughed. Tristan panted heavily. Once they were out, Charlemagne knelt down in the narrow corridor and checked the contents of his backpack to make sure they were alright. He then closed it and looked back at the kids.

"Ah, you see," Charlemagne remarked with a smile. "Swimming isn't so bad."

Tristan looked at him with a deep frown as he calmed down.

"What the hell is your problem?!" Tristan reacted. "Are you insane?! You just destroyed a two-thousand-year-old tomb!"

"Keep your voice down," Charlemagne hushed him, going over to him. "Hand me your radio."

Tristan looked at him with a puzzled look and gave him the radio.

"Johnathan, I need your help. Hello?" Charlemagne said.

"Mr. Cabernet! Where are you? What's going on? The guards are reacting to a loud noise we all heard along with a bit of seismic activity."

"Are the guards by the door?"

"Only one of them," Johnathan replied, "the other is doing a perimeter patrol.

"Right," Charlemagne replied, "I need you to distract that other guard – lead him to the entrance into the labyrinth."

"What? Are you sure?"

"Yes, you need to distract him. We're behind the door he's guarding."

"Alright – but what's going on? Are you alright?"

"I'm fine," Charlemagne replied. "The kids are alright. We just need to get going on the double!"

"Why?"

"Why?" Tristan questioned. "Because this maniac just destroyed an ancient long-lost tomb!"

"Oh, come off it!" Charlemagne shouted back at him. "You don't understand, Tristan – desperate times call for desperate measures. You have no idea of what I learned down there that justified destroying what was already thought to be lost."

"We could have just hidden it again?" Tristan argued.

"Hidden it? To let those crooks find it?" Charlemagne remarked, walking forward to the gate ahead.

"They weren't crooks! We could trust them!" Tristan countered.

"Oh, is that what you think?" Charlemagne replied, walking back over to them. "I suppose tracking us was a sign of goodwill too? Haven't you realized? There are tracking beacons on each of your backpacks."

"What?" Diana questioned, unlatching her backpack.

At the base of her backpack was a small flat disc. Diana removed it and dropped it into the sand. Tristan did the same and then looked to Charlemagne with embarrassment and fear.

"Let me tell you something, Tristan," Charlemagne lectured, walking over to him. "We are in no ordinary race. It is nothing like the races Diana competed in this spring. It is a dangerous, underground operation to secure one of the most dangerous artefacts in the existence of mankind. An artefact of which could provide unyielding power to the wrong person or set of people."

"What?" Tristan questioned. "What's so life-threatening or dangerous about a piece of jewelry."

"It is not about the necklace itself. It's about the stone and metal that make the necklace. The metal is the same light material that Johnathan and myself discovered in Giza – a metal of extraterrestrial origin that came of a meteorite that crashed here long ago as we saw in Abydos. The stone is… the same stone that I once searched desperately long ago… the same two orbs."

"And? What did the tomb say that confirmed all of this for you?" Tristan asked.

"The tomb… it confirmed not only the existence of the necklace, but also the existence of these mythical orbs. It explained their origin: the celestial orbs blessed upon the Nomarch of Thebes, Mentuhotep, which was drawn from the Nile and thought to also have originated from the Great Fireball meteorite if not another meteorite. The Egyptians called them the 'Atenakhet' and the 'Atenkku,' or the Season Disc and the Night Disc, or as I have come to refer to them, the Light Orb and the Night Orb. The possession of these artefacts gave Mantuhotep the determination to unite Egypt in the wars that came. It was under Amenemhat III, with the blessing of his Holy advisor, that one of them was crafted into a necklace to honor their friendship. The other was held by him. The Amulet of Ra as they called it – I assume, carries the Light Orb as Ra is the god of the sun. Regardless, I came to learn of these orbs from my old mentor, a former colleague of mine. He led an expedition into the Abu Simbel before it was submerged into the Lake Nasser. From Ramses II, he learned of the recovery of a special orb during his campaign in the Levant, stolen from the Hyksos Canaanites during their escape at the end of the Second Indeterminate Period and gifted to his wife. It was placed in Karnak Temple, while the other orb was described to be missing at the hands of traitorous king. The name of this king is unknown, although I have ruled out many candidates. I believe this orb to be our amulet."

"What's so dangerous about this orb though?" Tristan demanded to know.

"Well, various sources which mainstream scholars have discredited as ancient propaganda have told that there was once was a demi-god in the land of Egypt so powerful that he could not only control the flow of time, altering the seasons, but also teleport. The description of these powers matches what Pharaoh Ramses II described as 'dangerous powers' that these orbs hold. In addition, there is only one possible individual who could be this 'demi-god,' and that was the advisor of Amenemhat III – a man so powerful, yet both humble and wise. Of course, this man was the one that granted one of the orbs to Amenemhat III, becoming the Amulet of Ra, as I read in the tomb. We already discussed the possible identity of this man as being Joseph, son of Jacob, and/or Sinuhe from the Tale of Sinuhe, both of whom were powerful individuals and likely the same man. The connection of all this might be a coincidence, optimistic thinking, or whatever, but given the description of these orbs, one of which was said to be as dark as natural night, and another as bright as the sun, I question where they could have come from and what they can really do. It is no coincidence that fifty million dollars are being offered for the return of this amulet, which would contain the orb. I only fear the individual who knows all of this as I do, but I am now determined with absolute confidence that I will not allow this host to receive the amulet. I came into this race out of curiosity alone – the potential that it would lead me to these orbs when I saw a sketch of either of them in Sakharov's journal. However, my goals are set now. We cannot let anyone get their hands on this necklace and must secure it for the good of all that is good. Am I understood?"

Tristan looked at him with a serious face. He didn't say anything for a moment until he relaxed his fists.

"Charles, you're clear, get out of there," Johnathan radioed.

Charlemagne ignored him for a moment as he looked to Tristan.

"Yes, sir," Tristan forfeited.

"Good."

Act 3, Scene 5

Charlemagne sat around a campfire, writing in his journal with the sheet of paper he scribbled at his left side in the sand. Johnathan had left them to sure supplies in Faiyum, while Charlemagne thought it was a good idea to lay-low and do some camping. Tristan and Diana were in their tent as both were very tired from the events in Hawara.

In Charlemagne's journal, he had written a list titled 'Amenemhat III to Ramses II' with a long list of the names of kings and some names crossed out. One of the circled names was 'Akhenaten' with a brainstorm of ideas next to it, including 'Sun Disc monotheism' and 'but pillaged tomb.' At the bottom of the list were an assortment of auxiliary ideas, such as 'Narmer,' 'Khufu,' but these were scratched out. Another idea was 'Hyksos' with 'illegitimate rulers' next to it and 'but constrained to Lower Egypt' next to it.

Meanwhile, Tristan held Diana, who was fast asleep, and looked at the other end of the tent with a pensive face. He tightened his grip around Diana's body and shifted to a saddened face. Diana began to struggle as she tried to turn around in their sleeping bag, prompting Tristan to let go as Diana now faced him, burying her head into Tristan's chest. Tristan returned his arms around Diana, which caused her to open her eyes and look up.

"Are you still awake?" Diana questioned in a soft tone. "What's the matter?"

"Nothing," Tristan replied, touching his nose with Diana's. "I'm just thinking as usual. Don't worry about it."

"You're still upset about what Charles did, aren't you?"

"I think he might be losing it," Tristan warned. "I never thought he'd ever do something like that."

Diana lifted a soft smile and brought a hand to Tristan's cheek. The two kissed for a moment before parting.

Charlemagne raised his head up from where he was sat to look ahead at the kid's tent. His ears twitched from the sound of whispering from within, but before he could set his eyes back down onto his book, he was plunged into darkness as something came over his head. He struggled against it.

"What the hell?!" Charlemagne shouted. "What is this?!"

Diana and Tristan sat up in their sleeping bag. Tristan grabbed his shirt to put on while Diana grabbed a collared shirt to put over her t-shirt. Just as Tristan brought his shirt down over his stomach, the tent opened up to reveal the faces of two men in desert-grade army camouflage and gear. Diana immediately charged forward towards one of them, causing them to grab her and restraint her on the ground.

"Diana!" Tristan shouted, rushing after her.

Tristan was grabbed and thrown into the sand next to her. He looked to Diana next to him as they placed a bag over her head before the same fate was made of him.

Act 4, Scene 1

All that could be heard was the sound of sand meeting rolling tires. All three of them felt the sun against them as it rose from the horizon. Tristan had woken up from a short nap he had taken to feel his head poking into the hard flatbed of the vehicle he was on. His hands were tied behind his back, which added strain to his shoulder. He tried to calm down as he squirmed around but was met with the bashing of something hard into his stomach.

Charlemagne and Diana were also awake. Diana was on her knees, listening carefully to the sound around her, while Charlemagne, like Tristan, was on his side. He could feel a smooth plastic surface behind him that could touch with his hands alongside some loose rope from around his wrists. He played with it.

The vehicle came to a sudden stop and Tristan was picked up by his arms. Diana was pushed forward onto the ground before he was forced to stand. Charlemagne on the other hand was dragged and thrown overboard. The hoods came off from over the boy's heads, striking them temporarily blind as the sun shined into their eyes. Tristan shook his head before realizing he was standing in the back of a pickup truck. His eyes turned to the side where a man passed him to go towards Charlemagne with his duffel bag in his hand. The man dropped it down and removed the hoods while Tristan and Diana were forced onto their knees again.

"Where is it, Charles?" the man asked in an Eastern European accent, grabbing him by around the collar. "Where is old man Sakharov's book?"

"Attila?" Charlemagne questioned in a weak voice, squinting his eyes from the brightness around. "What... Why?"

Charlemagne looked at the man with tanned skin and long, light brown hair. He was dressed in similar camouflage and had similar gear to the others. He also wore black sunglasses to conceal his eyes.

"You know why, Charles, so answer to me so we can make this less painful and heartbreaking than it needs to be. Where is the book?"

"Go to hell..." Charlemagne replied.

"No, wrong answer. You see, Charles. We have your kids right here, and it's up to us whether we take them back to us to Cairo and drop them off at the Canadian embassy, or if they stay with you."

Charlemagne groaned as he looked over to where Diana and Tristan were. Diana was struggling with her ties, trying to get them loose while Tristan watched Charlemagne with a focused face.

"Give him the book, Charles," Tristan said to him.

"We've searched through all your things and can only find your journal," Attila remarked. "Where did you hide the other book?"

Tristan jerked his neck over to where a woman now walked from his right, carrying Tristan and Diana's backpack and bags. She threw them into the sand before crossing her arms.

"You're both a miserable lot, aren't you," Charlemagne said to them. "After all we've been through, you just stab me in the back. Is money that much of a value to you? Did I teach you nothing in all the years that we spent together? Tanya... you of all people too?"

"Okay," Attila responded, dropping Charlemagne and producing a baton.

"What is..."

Attila silenced Charlemagne with a strike in his side. He yelled out in pain before another stroke came.

"Stop! It's in his damn jacket! Just stop!" Tristan shouted.

Attila turned around and looked over to Tristan. He then put away his baton and opened Charlemagne's blazer, taking the book from within. He threw it to Tatiana and then left.

"I taught you better, Miko," Charlemagne yelled at him. "You would never be where you are now had it not been for me. Miklos!"

The man named Miklos went into the cabin of the truck and started the engine. Tatiana continued to look at Charlemagne, showing slight pity.

"Is that what you married? A monster that now kidnaps children?" Charlemagne taunted her.

"Tatiana! We're leaving!" Miklos shouted to her.

Tatiana turned around before she took a canister from her belt. She went over to Charlemagne and left it with him.

"I'm sorry," she said with a deep sigh, "if you're lucking, you might reach the closet village before anyone has to die."

"Tatiana!" Miklos shouted again.

Tatiana stood up and left. She hurried back into the cabin of the truck while Tristan felt his ties come loose from someone behind him. Diana felt the same as they were both set free and then pushed off from the back of the truth as it started to pick up speed.

"Wait! You can't abandon them too! They're only kids!" Charlemagne yelled out.

Tristan quickly stood up as he looked over to the truck leaving. Diana fell over and struggled to stand up since her ties were still not off yet. Tristan scowled at the truck as it parted, leaving them behind in the middle of a wide desert where the sun almost suffocated them in heat.

Diana finally got her ties off and was able to stand up. She looked around from side to side and felt sweat drop from her hair before she looked over to Charlemagne squirming around. Diana went over to help him.

Tristan turned around and looked at him. He then went over to pick up his backpack, searching through it to see what was left behind. Everything was there. Diana freed Charlemagne before she went to her own backpack. Charlemagne stood up and looked around.

The sand was smooth and pure around them, with minor dunes in the distance. The truck continued to drive off into the distant horizon, away from where the sun was rising. A mild breeze picked up, but it was hot and did not relieve the overwhelming heat.

Diana sat down in the sand and through her things. The kids were barefoot with Tristan wearing gym shorts and a t-shirt. Diana was in her underwear, t-shirt and collared shirt. Blood dripped from Charlemagne's face and into the sand.

Tristan looked to Diana and then he looked to Charlemagne who was still looking around. His feet started to burn from the hot sand, causing him to sit down and find his shoes. Diana stood up once she was dressed and began to look around hopelessly. Charlemagne rolled up his sleeves. He put the canister of water at his belt and separated his objects into two separate bags.

"Take only what you need with you," Charlemagne quietly said, standing up and bringing the strap of one bag around.

"Oh yeah, and where the hell are we even going?" Tristan asked him in a sarcastic tone, tying his shoes. "Do you even know where we are?"

"No, and I do not know where we are, but I do not intend to let you two just die out here," Charlemagne replied, walking forward in the direction the truck drove off in.

Tristan shook his head and stood up. Diana started to follow Charlemagne as they started their path forward. Tristan caught up to him and the two of them walked together towards a dune in the distance. At the very top, Diana looked over to the long stretches of desert ahead of them.

"Oh my God, we're actually going to die out here," Diana said.

"Don't say that," Tristan replied. "We survived the Russian cold and we'll survive the Egyptian heat."

"Your optimism won't save us," Diana responded, walking downhill to keep pace.

"Your pessimism won't either."

Diana took out a bottle of sunscreen lotion and started to protect herself before passing the bottle to Tristan.

"Do you want to give any to the old man?" Diana asked as Tristan finished.

"You hand it to him," Tristan replied. "I'm mad at him for wrecking that tomb – and for having us stranded in the desert where we're going to die."

"What happened to accepting the responsibility of the adventure?" Diana mocked.

Tristan didn't respond. They continued to walk as Diana went forward to offer Charlemagne the lotion. They took a break. Charlemagne stashed the extra canteen of water into his backpack and took out his own bottle. The kids each had their own too. The three of them rested for two minutes before they continued along.

The wind started to pick up and by noon, the sand started to trouble them as it ripped at their skin like snow in a blizzard. Tristan found his sunglasses and passed them to Diana, while Charlemagne continued onwards to lead them to the next dune.

At the top, nothing more could be seen except more sand. Diana took a deep sigh and started to go down for the next mile or two. Charlemagne continued to lead the way for them, but at the same time, as the sun started to make its descent into the afternoon, his legs shook and the vein at his forehead throbbed. His face was wet with sweat, which he tried to wipe with a handkerchief he had, but it had grown too wet and warm to provide much relief.

Tristan turned to Diana and could see that her fair skin was tanning and some parts had gone red. His own skin was dark – the darkest it had ever been in a long time. He grabbed the water bottle clipped to his belt and realized for the third time that it was empty as he tried to pour some water into his mouth. Diana's bottle was visibly empty too. Tristan started to slow down as he brought his hand to his forehead. Diana turned around to face him.

"What's up?" she asked.

"I'm... the heat. It's too much, Diana. My head hurts and I'm so damn hungry..."

Diana went over to him and took out a shirt from her backpack. She wiped Tristan's face with it and then took out a bit of rope that was used to tie her wrists earlier. She then took out her collar shirt and tied it around Tristan's head to provide some shade.

"Do you want your sunglasses back?" Diana asked.

Tristan shook his head as he looked down at the ground. Diana looked at him and took them off anyways. She put them on Tristan's reddened eyes and exposed her own to the brightness of the summer sun. Diana then kissed Tristan on his warm cheek before taking his hand so they could continue onwards to the next dune. She promptly let go and stuck to his side.

Charlemagne arrived at the top of the next dune and they continued downwards and onwards. Charlemagne's hands and knees continued to tremble as he looked ahead and then up to see that there was still a lot of day left before the sun would disappear.

The three of them continued and continued. They climbed the next dune and then climbed the next one. They crossed yards of sand only to see nothing ahead of them in the horizon.

By evening, the wind started to pick up and make it difficult to see much in front. The heat was starting to relieve itself even if it still felt too hot for comfort. Charlemagne marched up the latest dune when his body gave up. He fell face forward into the sand.

The wind ripped through Charlemagne's hair behind him and sand filled into it from the front. He brought his head up and felt shards of sand tear at his skin as he tried to look up. He started to crawl before coming to the top and collapsing his body. He then started to roll down the hill before hitting the side of something hard. He opened his eyes and looked up to see the top of a palm tree. His eyes widened with glee. However, he was too weak to move. His eyes closed again.

Charlemagne laid there, listening to the wind and crunch of sand as someone walked to him from nearby. Suddenly, he felt a wet towel placed over his forehead along with a gush of water falling into his mouth. He slowly opened his eyes and saw that the wind had stopped. It was evening and the man at his side had a masked face with goggles over the eyes. He removed the cover of his mouth and goggles to reveal his face.

The man looked similar to Charlemagne but was younger and had slight differences in his appearance. The man had longer grey hair and no moustache. Instead, he had a scruff of unshaven hair. His skin was the same fair tone, but the man was muscular.

He was dressed in professional gear, like a real explorer with a backpack with a spade on the side and a machete on the other side. He was armed with a revolver in a holster of his belt and knife at his lower legs.

"Grandad," Charlemagne muttered.

"Shhh…" the man hushed in an accent similar to his own, but deeper, removing the wet towel to change sides. "Save your strength, Charles."

"Your dead. You can't be real unless… oh God," Charlemagne moaned. "No…"

"You're not dead yet, son. You have work left to do on this world and have yet to recover the orbs."

"I… I can't. We're lost and I have no bloody clue where I'm supposed to go. I've doomed them. I've doomed the kids and now they're going to die because of me. After all that's happened thus far, I deserve this, but not them…"

"You've shown a great change of character over the past year, my dear boy," Derby said to him. "However, there is still much waiting for you to learn. The destruction of the tomb was a quick decision, but not the smartest you've made."

"What more was I supposed to do? What would you have done?" Charlemagne asked him. "I had no choice. I couldn't let sinister hands get their hands on the orbs."

"The kings and pharaohs – tyrants and saviors alike – have put their hands on the orbs to no effect as their powers are a myth said to only react in the hands of truly superior men. You've let fear guide your decision making – I would not have destroyed that tomb, but I would still have made it my duty to collect the orbs."

"I was selfish."

"Aye, you were," Derby replied.

"I was as selfish as Benito or Francisco were earlier, or worse yet, how Miklos was with me. I had no true reason to destroy that tomb other than to provide myself with a self-entitled lead in this race. I just... I need to find those orbs, grandad. I've searched for them for years and could not let them fall into someone else's hands."

"You of all people should know of the importance of preserving antiquity sites from the ancient world, Charlemagne. Has this land not suffered enough from the hands of greed? The hands of foreigners? The hands of the corrupt? You have a duty, Charles, to do what is right by your very blood. Follow through with it..."

"I will..." Charlemagne replied, closing his eyes.

"Charles...?" Derby said to him, shaking him.

Charlemagne didn't respond.

"Charles," a voice said again, shaking him.

"Charles!" Tristan shouted.

Charlemagne sprang to life as he woke up with a panic. Tristan jumped back in surprise.

"Children..." Charlemagne said, looking over to them. "What..."

"You passed out," Tristan explained. "I was worried you might have slipped into a coma or something."

Charlemagne produced the canteen of water. He offered it to the kids before he stood up. The sun was setting, but it was still hot out and dry. Tristan gave the water back to Charlemagne to drink.

"You need this more than we do," Tristan said to him. "Drink plenty."

Charlemagne nodded and took the bottle. He drank from it and then gave it to Tristan who gave it to Diana. She drank from it and then Tristan drank. The bottle was empty after Tristan drank at least a cup of water.

"Right…" Charlemagne said, taking a deep breath. "Onwards?"

Charlemagne led the couple forward, prompting Tristan to clip the bottle on his belt before he continued with Diana.

Another dune was at their feet, so they climbed up to reach the top where they could look out to what needed to be crossed next. Charlemagne had difficulty seeing so he took his binoculars from his backpack and looked out. Tristan and Diana joined him and sat down for another break. Tristan's stomach grumbled as all of them had spent the day fasting with no food.

Charlemagne focused his eyes on a strange object in the distance. It was circular or perhaps rectangular and seemed to be made of stone with a hollowed-center.

"Could it be?" Tristan whispered to himself.

"What?" Tristan asked, looking up to him.

"I believe I see a well," Charlemagne remarked, putting his binoculars away.

Charlemagne started to make his way down the hill and across the sand. He picked up his pace and began to run, reaching the structure within the next minutes to find a basin of water. Charlemagne brought his hands into the water and brought a handful to his lips. The kids joined him and took their bottles to fill them. Tristan then washed his face with Diana before they stopped to looked ahead as they heard the sounds of a chime nearby.

Act 4, Scene 2

Ahead was a lit structure made of stone. It was huge and had two-stories with a tower that stretched up double the height of the main structure. Its walls were white and had a short wall around it in the same smooth sandstone material as the outside. A pen could be seen attached on the side and trees on the outskirts with a pool of water – an oasis within the borders.

"Should we go?" Tristan questioned Charlemagne.

"We have to try," Charlemagne responded, standing up and picking up his backpack. "Come."

The couple followed Charlemagne for another short distance. They walked around the wall and found the gates of the structure and chime that had called them earlier. A sand road ran at the front of the home and stretched forward into the endless desert for what seemed to be many more miles. Charlemagne brought his hands around the steel bars of the gate and looked inside. It was not a modern home, but it still looked luxurious, nonetheless.

"Who would live all the way out here," Diana remarked with a frown.

"Who cares?" Tristan replied.

"Hello!" Charlemagne shouted. "Hello, we need help!"

"What are the chances whoever these people that they'd speak English?" Tristan said.

"Well, please help out if you know Arabic then," Charlemagne nagged.

Diana grabbed the strings of the chime and started to shake them, producing a loud and obnoxious orchestra of noise.

"Diana…" Charlemagne scolded.

"Hey, wait," Tristan replied, tapping Charlemagne on the arm. "Look."

Charlemagne jerked his head back forward where he heard and could see the door opening. It was a large wooden door. From within, a small hand came out and grabbed the edge of the door to peak out.

"Help, we need food, water, and shelter," Charlemagne asserted. "We've been lost and abandoned in the desert. We need help!"

The girl had fair tanned skin. She wore a black gown that went to her feet and she also wore a matching headdress that covered her hair. She turned around and spoke in an unknown language. The door widened to reveal two other people with her. They were dressed the same but varied in height. Each of them were quite young and did not appear to be like other locals the group had encountered thus far.

Each of them stood up straight and turned around as a fourth figure arrived. She was older and had the same kind of skin tone as the first girl. She wore a white headdress and gown instead. She also looked older but younger than Charlemagne. Her face was wrinkleless and regent like.

The younger girls said something to her before the woman in white said something to them whilst looking at Charlemagne and the kids. Whatever it was, it caused the three women in black to scurry down the path of the mansion and open the gates. The woman ushered them in and each grabbed an arm to bring them inside.

Charlemagne was in front and as he looked over to where the woman in white was, she was gone. They were brought into the foyer of the home, which was extremely cool and refreshing. It was well-decorated like a palace and had a canopy over an opening in the ceiling. Fixed torches were lit and brought a warm glow to the room.

The two girls ahead let go of them and rushed forward to a second pair of double doors on the right. They opened them and led the way for them to enter. It was a long room that stretched from one side of the house to the other. At the opposite end there was an open archway that looked out to the garden and pen behind. Curtains were pushed apart on either side and a gentle warm breeze floated in.

"Please, sit," one of the girls said as she passed them.

All three girls left them to go down the side of the large table and leave into a room at the far left. A dozen chairs were positioned on either side of the dining room with no chairs at the beginning or end. Charlemagne looked around. He went around and down close to the balcony. He set his belongings to his side.

"Oh, it feels so good to sit down in a chair after being on one's feet for so long," Charlemagne remarked.

The kids sat next to him and placed their belongings to their sides. In the next minute, a girl came out with a tray of vegetables, a pitcher of water, and three glasses. She set them down and poured the water.

"Thank you," Charlemagne said as she finished pouring his glass.

The woman poured Diana's and Tristan's before leaving the water in the center of the table and bowing. She then began to leave to Charlemagne's objection.

"Wait," Charlemagne said.

The girl did not stop and simply left. The kids helped themselves to cucumber, radish and leek before the door opened again with two other women about fifteen minutes later. One girl set them a plate and utensils while the other set the food down. Both of them bowed and then left them to eat.

Charlemagne did not object this time and simply let the kids and himself eat the *kusharni*, fish, and kebabs left for them. Each of them ate happily and did not talk throughout. Tristan stopped himself halfway through his meal as he noticed the door was slightly open at the opposite side of the room. He could see that he was being watched and he could hear whispers. The door closed, but Tristan was unsettled as he looked around suspiciously.

After they had finished, the woman came around again to take their plates and then leave. The door at the opposite-side of the room opened again, but the sound of voices talking in their unknown language was much obvious this time.

The woman in white entered the room with two maidens at her side. They were two new girls and they were much younger than the others. The woman spoke in their unknown language to the girls and they each went forward and put an arm around Diana and Tristan.

"What's going on?" Tristan questioned with a nervous laugh as he was forced onto his feet.

"Bath time," the woman in white replied in perfect English. "A bath to relax you with clothes waiting in our bathhouse for you to wear afterwards. Do not worry. We will take your clothing and have them washed for you to wear in the morning. A bed awaits you upstairs."

The woman smiled as the kids were guided around the table and out of the room, through the archway. She then looked to Charlemagne and stepped forward.

"I am most grateful for your hospitality, madame," Charlemagne said.

"Do not speak words that do not hold their meaning, Mr. Cabernet," she replied.

"You know who I am?"

"I do, and I know of someone that wishes to meet you in the morning, Mr. Cabernet. Until that time comes, you and your children are permitted to stay in our home. We have spare tunics waiting for you in the bathhouse as well. Leave your clothes there but take your possessions with you to your room.

Charlemagne nodded. The woman left and Charlemagne stood up. He picked up his belongings, went to the archway and looked over to another structure behind the main building. It was small and had a chimney extending from the roof.

Charlemagne jumped as he felt a hand around his arm. It was another woman in black. She guided Charlemagne to the bath.

Tristan was stopped at the entrance of the bath by a maiden, while Diana was permitted to pass. Diana turned around and looked to Tristan.

"I'll be quick," Diana replied. "I'll see you in a bit."

"Okay," Tristan responded, watching her go off with a saddened face.

Diana turned right, went down a corridor and came around to the bath. The room was large and had a shallow pool in the middle with steam floating up. The floor of the room was a grey stone. Columns protruded up at each lateral side and a doorway existed at the middle on one side with a fireplace at the other.

A maiden presented a basket and bowed to Diana. She set the basket by a stone bench and then left Diana to be on her own. She undressed herself and left her clothing in the basket.

Tristan sat down at a bench outside of the bathhouse. He then turned to an entrance into the main building of the convent. Charlemagne exited the building and went down the pathway towards the bathhouse.

"Is everything alright?" Tristan questioned him as he got close.

"Yes," Charlemagne responded, walking over and sitting down next to him.

"What is this place? What did that woman want?"

"She knows who I am," he replied. "And she said that there was someone that wanted to speak to me in the morning. After all that's happened, I'm a bit weary and skeptical of all this, so be careful. Where is Diana?"

"She's bathing," Tristan replied.

"Right," Charlemagne responded. "We're in a vulnerable state and they could use that to their advantage."

"What are we going to do then?"

"Just be careful," Charlemagne responded.

Tristan nodded and then went silent. A minute passed before Tristan looked to his guardian again.

"Charles, what language were they speaking? It didn't sound like Arabic, and that woman in white was able to speak English perfectly."

Charlemagne gave a sigh and then turned to Tristan and said, "I believe they were speaking Ancient Greek."

"Ancient Greek?" Tristan questioned.

"I'm equally perplexed as you are," Charlemagne responded, looking around with shifting eyes. "The other possibility is Latin, but with the exception of the Vatican State, no other sovereign state that I'm aware of uses the language. It wouldn't surprise me if somehow these people were connected to either the Church, the Roman people, or both – now that I think of it, this bathhouse is quite Roman. I have never really heard either language spoken and their accent could be either or."

Tristan looked around. Diana exited the bathhouse wearing a white dress that went to her ankles. The tunic dress looked Greco-Egyptian and left her arms exposed with straps that went around her collar bone. A white rope wrapped around her waist. Diana's hair was still wet but wrapped around her neck. She also wore white sandals.

126

"Diana," Charlemagne said, "are you alright?"

"Yeah," Diana replied, walking over to them. "I'm feeling refreshed as well."

The maiden at the entrance of the bathhouse walked over to Diana and brought an arm around hers. She then led her away from the kids and back towards the house.

"I'll see you in the morning, I guess," Diana said to them.

"Be careful," Charlemagne replied.

Tristan didn't say anything to her and instead watched her off. The two then walked towards the entrance of the bathhouse and came around to the actual bath.

"I've never seen such a big bathtub," Tristan said as he stood at the entrance.

"Yes, this is quite Roman," Charlemagne replied, looking around.

Tristan looked over to a maiden in black as she picked up a basket with Diana's clothing. Near the basket were two other baskets for the kids to use. She took the basket and then gave the kids some privacy.

Tristan undressed himself as soon as the maid left them. He put his clothes in the basket and looked to a bench where there were stacks of towels for them. Next to the bench was a wooden table with a plate of wrapped soap. Tristan took a bar, walked over to the bath and entered one step at a time until he was waist-deep.

"Wow, that's hot... but not too hot."

Charlemagne entered the bath after he had undressed himself and set his clothing in the basket next to Tristan.

"I made a grave mistake in Hawara," Charlemagne confessed, looking at the mist over the water before looking at Tristan. "I want you to know that I realize what I did in the pyramid was inappropriate and horribly unethical."

Tristan looked back at him from the other side of the bath. He did not reply. Charlemagne began to tell him about what happened to him when he passed out – that he saw his grandfather. When he was finished, each of them took a moment of silence.

"I was extremely fortunate to have the grandfather that I had," Charlemagne remarked "Even though I know that my hallucination of him was just a hallucination – an expression of my subconscious, it unsettles me to know that I did what I did. I'm sorry not only to you, because I know that I upset you, but to all those that will no longer be able to learn and enjoy what was in that tomb."

"There's lots in history that has been lost, and it's a tragedy that such is true, but don't beat up yourself too much over it because the matter of fact is that it wasn't a great travesty," Tristan finally replied. "I'm not mad at you."

"Thank you," Charlemagne replied, nodding to him.

Silence broke out between the two again. Charlemagne cleared his throat.

"Well, I'm exhausted over the events of today and should get some rest. Apparently, I have a meeting with an unknown individual, who hopefully can help us get back to civilization."

"Right," Tristan replied, looking down into the water.

Charlemagne exited the bath, dressed himself and left Tristan behind. Charlemagne took his belongings with him as he exited and went back to the main building. Tristan remained in the water, relaxing and tilting his head back until he heard the sound of someone entering. He jerked his head over to the entrance and saw who it was.

"Diana," Tristan said, looking at her before giving a soft smile. "You look like a Greek goddess in that dress."

Diana blushed. She walked over to where Tristan was and then sat down on the ground with her legs at her side.

"Is everything alright?" Tristan asked her.

"Yup," she replied, looking at him. "One of the girls showed me to my room, but as much as I am tired, I couldn't think to sleep without seeing you beforehand."

Tristan smiled at her and then turned his body so that he could rest his arms on the rim of the bath. She ran her hands through his wet hair.

"Aren't you going to wash yourself?" Diana questioned.

"I'd rather talk."

"About?"

"Anything, but I am tired," Tristan replied. "I also expect that we'll be sleeping in separate beds tonight, so I'm a little upset over that."

"You'll survive."

Diana picked up the package of soap that Tristan had left on the side of the bath. She then opened it and revealed the pinkish brick. She dunked it into the water and then began to expose her hands to the soap. From there, she began to wash Tristan's hair. Once she was done, he dunked himself into the pool and then re-emerged, shaking his hair.

"I feel cleaner already," Tristan said, looking at Diana.

Tristan took the bar of soap from where Diana had left it and then began to wash his torso and neck, rubbing the soap over his gold chain necklace with his amulet of a saint. He then washed his arms before submerging himself up to the bottom of his head. Tristan continued to clean himself before leaving the bar of soap where Diana had placed it. He then brought himself into the water before walking out to grab a towel. Diana stood up and went over to embrace Tristan once he was dried and had the towel around his waist. The couple shared a passionate kiss.

Diana and Tristan were quick to part at the sound of a gasp from the entrance. They both turned to see one of the maidens had walked in on them. She held a vase jar in her hands and looked embarrassed. She quickly left, which caused Diana to bring herself into Tristan's arms.

"Welp," Diana responded.

"Welp?" Tristan replied, holding her. "Oh God, what if we get kicked out for that... Do you think that's frowned upon?"

"It's probably best if we split up and go to our separate rooms," Diana replied, parting from and going to grab some clothing for Tristan. "Here."

Tristan put on the tunic which went to his knees. He then fastened the leather belt around his waist.

"Wow, this feels more comfortable than I envisioned," Tristan remarked, drying his hair with his towel. "Aren't you going to say that I look like a Greek god or even a warrior?"

"Hm, not a chance, Achilles," Diana replied, walking past him and grabbing his hand. "Come on, let's go."

Tristan put his arm around Diana, and the two slowly made their way out of the bathhouse.

"You know," Diana remarked, "I was promised that there would be some camping. Since we were interrupted last night, we have yet to do some camping."

"If you're so eager to camp, we could always camp out behind the manor."

"Hm, I'll think about that," Diana replied.

The couple walked out of the bathhouse but stopped as they stepped outside. At the top of the steps going into the main building was the woman in white. The couple parted from each other and dropped their smiles as they saw her looking at them. The two then walked towards her. She opened the door for them.

"You may follow me to your room, young boy," the woman said, stepping forward.

Tristan looked at her and then over to Diana. The two parted as Tristan followed the woman upstairs. She led him to a door, opened it and then allowed him to enter. Inside, Tristan's belongings were left atop of a chest at the foot of a bed. He looked forward and then turned around to the other side of the corridor where past the railings.

The room was small, but had a private washroom, which was in itself small and only contained a toilet and sink. The room did contain a large window to the left of the bed, which looked out to the desert oasis.

Diana found herself in a similar room, but on the ground floor and on the opposite side of the room. Her room looked out to the desert dunes. She sat down at a divan at the base of the window and frowned. Her arms displayed goose bumps, which caused her to stand up and go to the bed. She wrapped herself in a blanket and then fell asleep.

Act 4, Scene 3

In the morning, Charlemagne was brought into a study on the ground floor. The office was small and had a glass window at the opposite side from the door. In front of the window was a desk with a man behind it. He was dressed in a black cassock. He also wore a clerical collar that poked out at the top. He had curled white hair, bushy beard and tanned skin that he covered with a black headdress with a black cloth stretched out back. He looked to be in his sixties, had wrinkles, and wore thick circular glasses. He was average height.

The woman in white led Charlemagne into the office as the man rose from his desk. He lent a hand to a chair with a smile.

"Please, Mr. Cabernet, take a seat," he said in perfect English. "I am Patriarch Antioch of Alexandria, Provincial Superior of *Aigyptos* for the Order of St. Athanasius."

"Patriarch?" Charlemagne replied, taking a seat.

The woman in white left the room and closed the doors for them. The patriarch sat down and put his hands together, resting them atop of the desk with a straight posture.

"I have heard of your presence in Egypt, but did not expect us to ever meet. I have asked myself, 'What business does a billionaire have in this land?' After all, what does a man like yourself seek in another fifty million dollars – that must be pocket change to a man like you."

"Are you and this convent the host of the underground race? Or perhaps the Church?"

"The Church?" the Patriarch questioned. "No, Mr. Cabernet. Neither I nor the Church are in relation to this quest. And I know that you are not here for a simple relic."

The door opened behind them. Charlemagne's ears twitched as the woman in white entered the room again with a briefcase.

She set it down at the side of the desk and then left. The man ignored her. Charlemagne raised a frown.

"Tell me, why do you seek the orbs of Ra and Osiris?"

"I don't know what you are talking about."

"Mr. Cabernet, you cannot lie to me. We are on the same page."

"Did you send those mercenaries after us?"

"I know nothing of that sort. You are here by pure chance, I assure you."

Charlemagne looked at the patriarch with skepticism. He slouched back in the chair.

"You seek my trust before we can talk in detail?" the patriarch asked, turning in his rotating seat as he parted both hands. "I suppose that is only logical. A stranger never trusts another stranger no less in a foreign land."

"Where am I?"

"You are in the Convent of the Sisters of St. Catherine on the Sinai Peninsula."

"Can I assume this is an Orthodox monastery then?" Charlemagne questioned.

"No, you cannot," the patriarch responded. "Nor can you assume that it is a Roman Catholic one or even protestant."

"What language are the nuns speaking?"

"The language spoken in this house is the survival of the Egyptian language known as Coptic. You see, this monastery was founded long ago in the days of Byzantium Empire, and even throughout the Arabic and Turkic conquests, it has stayed loyal and true to only Christ and God. It was protected by an ancient order that has attempted to prevail in the face of schism and reformation, revolution and decline. Most of the women here are of distant Greek ancestry from throughout Egypt to live here in harmony before they can blossom into mothers, but let's not talk about them. Let us talk about these orbs that you seek and our mutual interest in them."

"What interest do you have in the orbs?"

"I have the sole interest to safeguard them, you see, since the beginnings of the universe billions of years ago there has existed those that oppose all that is good – the beauty and the sublime. Today, the agents of evil exist as minions that pour over from the nearby border with blood lust – funded by the Children of Moloch."

"You've lost me," Charlemagne confessed.

"Bad people, Mr. Cabernet," the patriarch clarified. "Bad people seek the orbs, and while they may be both primitive and simple-minded, their nefariousness knows no ends and even in the simplest of creatures, these orbs can still be dangerous weapons."

Charlemagne's eyes widened.

"Alright then," Charlemagne replied. "I understand somewhat that we have similar goals, but how can I know that your intentions aren't nefarious as well."

"My sole intention is that you secure those orbs."

"And so I secure the orbs, and then you take them?"

"In order to protect them."

"I don't trust you."

"We have suspicions of you as well, Mr. Cabernet."

"Me?" Charlemagne questioned.

"Our informants have already told us of what has occurred in Hawara – Giza."

"I was mistaken and blinded by my own vices."

"Tell me, what sort of leads do you have in regard to the orbs?"

"Well, none anymore," Charlemagne simply replied. "The majority of my notes were stolen during the kidnapping last night."

"What kidnapping?"

"My children and I were kidnapped at our camp in Faiyum and we were searched for all the information I possessed. They took with them an important book that led me to the Hawara pyramid, and with that, a lot of my personal research and documentation from over the years. After that, we were thrown into the (I suppose, Sinai) desert until we found ourselves here."

"What book did you have?"

"An old book, or journal, that belonged to an old colleague of mind. He was part of an expedition that was never completed."

"What expedition?"

"An expedition put together by Dr. Maxim Ivanov from the University of St. Petersburg."

"Dr. Ivanov is dead. He was a colleague of both me and another man interested in this field – Provincial Superior Tristan Williamson of Albion, our British chapter, or as he was publicly known as, Bishop Williamson. Unfortunately, Bishop Williamson is also dead."

"My colleague also died approximately two weeks ago," Charlemagne remarked in a saddened tone.

"Right, but we are getting sidetracked. Where do you think the Amulet of Ra is located?" the patriarch asked, turning forward in his chair and leaning over with his hands together.

"I don't know. All I could surmise was that it was buried with a 'traitor' that existed between the reign of Amenemhat III and Ramses II."

"What brought you to that conclusion?" the patriarch questioned, picking up a briefcase at his feet and putting it on the desk.

"Some earlier research of mine… the research that drew me to find the orbs in the first place came from Abu Simbel before it was scuttled. It said that the amulet, or stone, which was part of the amulet, had been lost to a traitor. I learned in Hawara that Amenemhat received this stone from an advisor of his, so this is all I have to go on in regards to the time frame. In my own opinion, the Hyksos or Akhenaten are the most likely candidates."

"Yes," the patriarch agreed, nodding as he opened the briefcase. "I would say that those two are very good guesses. Akhenaten possessed by Baal, or Ra, idolized the Sun, and the Hyksos were vile people with no respect for Egyptian culture who stole from the people. However, I'm afraid to say that both are wrong answers. You search for a man or group of men, Charlemagne, but it was neither that Ramses referred to, but a woman."

"A woman? Hang on – do you know where the amulet is?"

"When Christianity first came to Egypt, many ancient artefacts and temples of the pagan religion were destroyed in goodwill as these were the artefacts of the Devil, and in this crossfire, a wealth of knowledge and culture was lost. The Great Library – a bastion of information and knowledge – was burned to the ground as was so much elsewhere that was precious to Egyptian culture and heritage. However, prior to their conversion to Christianity, the god worshipped as Ra, or Amun-Ra later, was the same god worshipped by the Canaanites known as Baal, Baal-Hammon, or better known as Moloch, or a more relevant term would be the Devil himself, but that term is too muddled. All that was a tribute to this idol of theirs was destroyed because they were demonic figments as material worship is. The pantheon of Egypt is directly related to the pantheon of Canaan, which is coincidentally related to the pantheon of Hinduism. Likewise with the culture, such is with the people; the Egyptian people have not existed for centuries to say. The best approach to history is to put yourself in the time period as a whole – for example, if we were to place ourselves in the middle of what we refer to as the Old Kingdom, we would need to consider the demographics of this period, who and what kind of people walked these lands and neighboring lands, because it is easy to assume that all of ancient Egypt was the same since the pre-dynastic periods. Or even who we refer to as Egyptians as being the same people. We need to remember that in these ancient times, less people existed than today. In addition, in relation to Caucasoids, the genetic relation of the three branches was closer than at the start of the common era because this was the period of divergence."

The patriarch paused for a moment to clear his throat.

"Are you familiar with the story of Noah?"

"Of course," Charlemagne replied.

"Noah had three sons…" the patriarch said.

"Shem, Japheth, and Ham," Charlemagne answered. "And these three brothers were believed to be the patriarchs of the three different *races* if you will, of Caucasoids: Semites, Japethites, and Hamites. Ancient Egyptians being believed to be descendants of Ham. I'm sorry, but what is the relevance of this?"

"The scholarship of the order has estimated the Great Flood to have occurred approximately at the start of the First Indeterminate Period with changing climate being a contributing factor to the conditions that caused the decline of the Old Kingdom."

"The flood was a flood, but the opposite – droughts, were believed to have caused the decline of the Old Kingdom," Charlemagne corrected.

"Floods in the Levant from the Gulf to the Caucasus could mean droughts in Egypt. After the floods, the sons of Noah went out and multiplied, and from there it is believed that Ham populated the lands of Egypt and Canaan to become the forefather of the Egyptians and Canaanites; Canaanites would later become the Edomites, Phoenicians, and Carthaginians, and then these would carry on in their own manner to the ends of the world. Not all the people of the world went extinct due to the floods, but surely, there were great casualties in the centralized location of the floods where in these areas extinction of the local populations occurred – for this was the center of our old world. In addition, the people of Sub-Sahara Africa and East Asia went about their business, and likewise the local population of Egypt, although struggling with the flood, went about theirs. After the flood, it is possible that these people became one with the descendants of Ham through a bottleneck effect. And then came the Assyrians, the Persians, and finally the Greeks and Romans who invaded. Do you know what all these people have in common?"

"Noah? If this is all true, what of before the flood? Who were Egyptians beforehand? There existed a pre-dynastic period and people beforehand, so who were they?"

"Prior to the flood, their lineage could be less certain – the land was inhabited by Proto-Caucasoids that have lived from up to 10,000 B.C., from whom this ancient religion derives from. These same people lived from the Indus Valley region to the Nile, but in this land of Egypt, they found themselves in contact with what were a people related to Australoids of South India and Australia, who they assimilated with. The evidence of this assimilation is seen by the depictions of the people in statues as well as the morphological features in remains. This group of people were none other than the descendants of Cain, and in the First Indeterminate Period, many of them perished in the droughts. Those that remained existed south to form Kush, while others in Egypt would have assimilated with what were the descendants of Ham. For centuries, Egypt, like Ham and Cain, has been cursed, and their curse was to be invaded and to exist in this state of abomination, being the Israelites' ransom for their liberation once at the slaying of the firstborns, and twice as a tribute to Cyrus to free them from Babylon. Only the Babylonians, who were also the sons of Ham had ravaged Judah and expelled all but the Judahites from Israel, but does Babylon or the Babylonians exist? No. It remains that Egypt is a cursed land – even before the Assyrians, Egypt had been invaded by the Kushites, and after the Romans it enjoyed a peace under Byzantium until the Arabs and Turks took over."

The patriarch took a moment to sigh.

"And these women... who are they?" Charlemagne questioned. "I don't believe them to be Egyptian."

"It would be impossible for them to be genuinely Egyptian, as there has been so many variants of Egyptian over the years, it would be difficult to settle on which is the foremost Egyptian – the most Egyptian of the Egyptians. The current government claims that the people as they are, are the same as the people of then – an outlandish claims. No, while the people of Egypt truly represent the modern Egyptian, the women of this convent, with their beauty, are of the descendants of an old noble family of a man named Yuya, whose daughter was the mother of Akhenaten. From their blood, lies ancient Egyptian customs, culture, and Egyptian life – in a sense of the word, they are who this Order believe to harness the essence of the Egyptian people, and also chosen to preserve and protect. They are fluent in both Coptic and Greek rather than Arabic – Coptic being the most genuine of the Egyptian languages, and Greek a mark of their spiritual and other blood ancestry that has provided and allowed the preservation of their cultural tradition rather than it be destroyed as it is now. Nonetheless, the tradition they practice is theirs. It is by their ancestral rite that they represent the closest link to the past, by their blood, and worship the one true apostolic faith rather than Islam or worse, paganism. All they hold has been lost in the modern Egyptian and modern Egypt."

The patriarch paused for a moment.

"The state government of people who call themselves Egyptian and claim the culture and history of the past as theirs are careless. It is understandable when one understands that these people in government are not genuinely *Egyptian* as the girls of this convent are. And this is not simply the case of only Egypt, but also of other countries in the Middle East that have suffered by the destructive Turkic and Arabic invaders. It is the duty of my office to preserve this past and conserve what is good – what God has made. After the failure to put together Dr. Ivanov's expedition, we sought alternative means. Behold."

The patriarch opened the briefcase to reveal a necklace inside with a slick chain and dark black gem detached from the top with a holder that trapped it within.

"My God, is that it?" Charlemagne questioned, looking at it with fragile eyes.

"No, it is an extremely well-crafted replica made of silver and an expensive black diamond. It is much heavier than the original."

The patriarch closed the case and set it aside.

"The original is where we found it – a place we deemed to be safe until now. The Amulet of Ra is hidden in the sublevel of the Temple of Queen Hatshepsut, which brings me to what I require of you. You are concerned of the several groups rummaging around this land in search of the amulet to hand it to a greedy collector, but I am worried of a particular group destroying all that is before them with wrath and malice where one should find a heart."

Charlemagne nodded.

"Thus, I propose a partnership where I will offer you resources, the means to travel to Luxor, and access to the sublevels in return for the amulet to be brought to us and kept safe."

"What does safe mean?"

"It will be stored in a vault where it can remain hidden until the time is right where it can at least be researched if not placed in appropriate hands."

Charlemagne didn't immediately respond until he said, "Why do you need me? Why not send one of your agents to do it if you have so many resources?"

"The mission is too important to hire a stranger, and there is nobody else that we do not trust."

"Grant me permission to conduct personal research on the artefact and then we have a deal. It has been my passion for decades to learn the truth of this orb, and I won't let it be forgotten in some vault."

"Very well, but only under our supervision, Mr. Cabernet," the patriarch replied. "A car awaits you outside to take you and your children back to Cairo. There, you will be contacted and given the necessary supplies and intel to travel to Luxor. Pleasant travels, Mr. Cabernet. Good luck."

Act 4, Scene 4

"I wonder what the hell happened Johnny," Tristan said as they drove through a canyon on a sandy asphalt road.

"I worry too, but we don't have time right now to investigate. I'm sure he is fine."

Charlemagne drove their van from Luxor and parked it in the small empty parking lot before the long path to the temple. The Mortuary Temple of Queen Hatshepsut was three stories tall and extended a path from the parking lot, up two ramps to reach the top. The exterior of the temple had columns along the wall. The structure was rectangular in shape with small rectangular floors stacked on top. It was all neatly built behind a straight cliff.

"An interesting face about this temple is that straight from this road, going back into town and across the Nile, you'll come to the Karnak Temple we saw from the hotel," Charlemagne said, turning around and pointing back. "The tomb was designed to face it."

"Sounds convenient," Diana replied, looking at the long path in front of them.

Charlemagne went around to the back of the van and opened it up. He pulled out the briefcase and opened it. Diana came around to get her backpack and Tristan his. Charlemagne gently picked up the necklace and looked at it.

"It's nice," Tristan remarked.

"It didn't look at I expected it to look," Charlemagne said, lowering it as he looked at Diana. "Here, keep this safe in your backpack."

Diana took off her backpack and opened it up. Charlemagne deposited the necklace and then closed the van.

"Where is everyone?" Tristan questioned.

"We have the entire place to ourselves," Charlemagne replied. "Between the recent terror warnings and the patriarch's power to have security dissipate from this area, I suppose he has proven we might just be able to trust him."

The trio started their trek down the path, but instead of climbing up the first ramp, Charlemagne diverted to the ground floor to follow the instructions handed to him on cue cards. He walked diagonally across and entered underneath the structure, past the columns, and down to the very far right. A blank door stood there. Charlemagne took out a key from his pocket and unlocked the door. It opened to reveal a dark room.

Charlemagne waited at the door, took out a flashlight and stuck it into the pocket of his blazer to light the way forward. He then entered the room and let the kids in. On the far-left was another door, but his one was semicircular and had a wide double-door.

"All of this must have been implanted during the rebuilding. I can only imagine what lies ahead," Charlemagne said as he went to unlock the second door.

"Me too," Tristan replied, looking forward.

"Well, I say that," Charlemagne said as he retracted the key, "but I doubt we could expect any sort of traps."

"How reassuring," Diana remarked, crossing her arms. "Does that book they gave you say anything about traps."

"Err… it doesn't specify any. All it says is to be careful in vague words," Charlemagne replied, opening the doors.

The doors revealed a long semicircular tunnel that went into the darkness.

"Besides, I wouldn't worry too much," he added, stepping inside. "The New Kingdom wasn't known for adding traps to their tombs, only elaborate mechanisms like the ones we've seen thus far to hide the true treasure. We can probably expect something along those lines."

"Well," Tristan replied, taking a deep sigh. "Let's get to it then."

Tristan led the way forward, prompting Charlemagne and Diana to walk after him. About three meters into the corridor, Tristan felt his shoe dig into the ground as the stone at his feet inserted downwards.

"Huh?" Tristan questioned with alert.

It was too late. He pushed the force of his right leg into the false floor, causing it to collapse at his feet. Charlemagne and Diana were ready to respond by immediately grabbing him and pulling him backwards. Charlemagne looked down at the ground at the deep pit that had appeared where the bricks were.

Tristan was panting as Charlemagne let go to step forward and investigate. Diana kept hold of him as they both calmed down.

"No traps, eh?" Tristan remarked, looking over to Charlemagne as he got Diana to let go.

"I'm sorry, but I didn't expect this... it's not part of the M.O. for this era."

"The stupid book and that priest could have warned us about collapsing floors!" Tristan complained.

"We'll have to jump across," Charlemagne said, standing up and looking over. "It's a small gap – come along."

Diana and Tristan looked at each other before they looked over to Charlemagne.

"You first," Diana said.

Charlemagne swung his arms and made a leap over the pit. He landed on the stable ground on the other side and began to continue to walk forward with careful steps, examining the stone slabs as though they were thin ice.

"You need to stop falling to your death," Diana said to Tristan.

"Sorry, I'll try harder not to die," Tristan replied, looking back at her.

"Come on over, children," Charlemagne said. "We'll need to cross together and keep each other's backs."

"Let's go," Tristan said, going over to make his leap.

Diana and Tristan rejoined Charlemagne who had taken out some rope. He tied some of the rope through his backpack and belt before he got the kids to do the same.

"I'll lead with caution. If I fall, it's up to you two to make sure I don't meet my end," Charlemagne explained. "Understood?"

"Yes, sir," Tristan replied.

"Good."

Charlemagne continued forward, tapping his feet hard into the stone to see if he could push any slabs down. Within five meters from the last, he managed to create a dent in the floor.

"Ahah," Charlemagne said, withdrawing his foot. "We've got another trap here."

"How the hell is anybody supposed to know about this?" Tristan questioned. "I mean, you step into one slab, you're dead. How are visitors supposed to come in?"

"I doubt this tomb was meant for visitors," Charlemagne replied. "It's more to do with keeping thieves at bay."

"How did the others get through then?" Diana asked. "I mean, one person comes in, falls, dies, but that only warns the second looters who'll be more cautious."

"Sometimes there are people who are paid in advanced to replace these mechanisms, so the floor will be replaced by the time a second thief can come around. Think of it like an intrusion alarm – the guards of this temple would notice the forced entry and put in an order to reset the trap. Since the initial thief is dead, he cannot go back and warn others of the trap. I know, it has its flaws, but it's still practical for its time."

"That priest could have still warned us," Tristan remarked.

"How are we going to jump with this rope keeping us together?" Diana asked instead.

"We're not going to jump. We're going to keep to the wall and keep our weight off the center piece," Charlemagne said. "Come."

Charlemagne pressed his stomach onto the wall and started to edge his way across. He focused the weight of his toes on the floor closest to the wall, gently moving across until he was a good distance to check if he was safe. The kids followed and after kicking his heel back and being sure it was stable ground, he stepped back and continued just like that.

At the end of the tunnel there was a set of stairs that went up to an enclave. Charlemagne tapped his hands on the surface and looked around at it.

"Looks like a false wall," Charlemagne said.

"There's a lever here," Tristan noticed, standing to the right a couple feet back.

Charlemagne turned around and went over. He examined it and started to untie the rope around him and the kids. He then put his hands over the lever.

"Should we spread out? In case… something falls on top of us or something," Tristan suggested.

Charlemagne looked around.

"Go, stand at the base of the stairs," Charlemagne warned.

The couple did that before Charlemagne pulled the lever. The stone slabs that were blocking the path simply rose, showing his way into the next corridor.

"Alright, it's clear," Charlemagne said, looking down the steps. "Come back over."

The kids regrouped and together they walked into the next room. Charlemagne stepped into a soft stone again, which prompted the stone behind them to drop back down.

"Oh, great," Diana replied.

Charlemagne looked behind him as he panted after his fright. He then turned back forward to look at what was before them. It was a small pool of water that went to the opposite end.

"More trap floors?" Tristan questioned. "These people are pretty unoriginal."

Charlemagne put a foot in the murky water. It was cold and caused him to withdraw from it immediately. He could see at the other end of the room was a similar enclave blocked by a stone slab with another lever. He took another step into the water and with confidence, walked towards the opposite end.

"If there were any false floors in this room, the water would have dripped through by now," he explained.

Charlemagne led the way forward. The water went only to their ankles. He stopped them in the middle where squared island was inserted into the pool, raising them up slightly in the water. He could not see anything special in the stone, so he continued forward to the opposite end so they could get out of the pool. He shined his light up to some hieroglyphics above the enclave and then looked over to the door. He put his hands to the lever and pulled it down. It did nothing.

"What does this say?" Tristan asked, looking at the ancient symbols.

"One moment," Charlemagne replied, patting his hands on the stone slab in the front of them.

Charlemagne then took a step back and went to read the hieroglyphics. Diana looked at the statues at either side of the enclave as he did so. He then looked back into the large corridor and shined light at the sides where a mural was painted on both sides. Each side was the same.

"It says… 'the answer is in the water' or 'the answer is from the water…' that's the best I can muster," Charlemagne remarked, looking over to the kids.

Charlemagne looked to Diana who was looking at the walls on the side. He went to join her.

"So, do we search in the water for some sort of answer?" Tristan asked. "Is this a quiz? Or is there a key in the water? A switch?"

"I'm not sure…" Charlemagne replied.

Charlemagne went back into the water to go to the start of the mural. He followed it from the beginning where a princess was bathing in water on a sunny day. It then showed a child in the water, and the child coming to the woman. The princess gave the child to a servant before the next scene split up. Above, the woman was behind a prince and behind them were two other princes and a princess. All five of them were behind one king. The sun shined above the first princess. Below, the son was now an Egyptian noble. In the next scene, the son was attacking someone, another noble. The pharaoh was leading the charge of some soldiers while the princess was saddened. In the scene afterwards, the princess was married with her brother above, while below it, it showed the son on his knees.

The second-last scene showed the son with a walking stick against the new pharaoh and the mother. In the last scene, it showed the king drowning while below it, it showed the mother as the pharaoh.

Charlemagne paused for a moment to give a thought before he looked back over to the statues. The statues were not of Hatshepsut. They were of a male figure whose face was bearded.

He looked above him to see if there was something in the ceiling, but there was nothing.

"Well?" Tristan questioned.

Charlemagne continued to think before he went over to one of the statues. He put his arms around it to see its weight.

"Help me move this," Charlemagne said.

Tristan helped him and together they caused the statue to tip over into the water. They then pushed it towards the center where Charlemagne wanted it. They tipped it back up and got it in the middle. They then trudged back over to the door where Charlemagne put his hands on the lever.

"Please stay in the water," Charlemagne said to the kids, "in case this backfires."

Once the kids were in the water, he pulled the switch and the door rose. The three of them walked through and entered a squared room. Charlemagne stepped on another pressured slab that caused the door behind them to shut. They entered the room where a sarcophagus sat in the middle. It did not have a lid and was empty.

"Right, let's split up and look for any possible false walls," Charlemagne said, looking around the room.

The trio did that and looked around. Diana found a crack in the wall in less than two minutes. The three of them then pushed against the wall to cause it to spin open, revealing a small room with a ladder going upwards to another level.

"Well, that was easy," Diana said, looking into the tomb.

The three of them had entered another squared room, but one with objects of gold, wooden chests, and various other treasures around. A sarcophagus was placed in the middle, sealed. It was decorated.

Charlemagne entered the circular room and looked around. He looked at the walls which showed various artworks and writings. He then looked over to the sarcophagus, which was beautifully decorated and had a golden cast. The face of the pharaoh was like the statues in the former room, but more colorful with its golden surface. The blue eyes had shadow underneath and depicted the pharaoh as clean-shaven with a firm jaw. Charlemagne brought his fingers underneath the cover and tried to lift it, he managed to lift the cover, revealing a mummy inside.

"Curious," Charlemagne remarked, gently lowering the cover onto the opposite side of the casket.

Charlemagne looked at the corpse. Its face was similar to the casket.

"Right, the necklace isn't with the body, so it must be around this room. Help me search."

Charlemagne went to some of the treasures around and started to look. None of them could find it. He picked up a golden necklace and began to examine it. He noticed its light weight and dropped it onto the ground.

"Some of these items aren't gold," Charlemagne said. "They're too light to be gold – I shouldn't have been able to lift that sarcophagus cover on my own, for example. The items in this room are made of pyrite – fool's gold."

"So?" Diana questioned. "We were tricked."

"No," Charlemagne refused. "Search the walls. Look for another opening," Charlemagne remarked. "The patriarch would not have given us an expensive replica and sent us to a dead-end. It's here somewhere."

The three of them began to examine the walls, but this time, Charlemagne found a crack for them to follow. They pushed against the wall, causing the wall to turn on an axis similar to the hidden doorway in Hawara. The door only went so far before crashing into the wall behind it. It led into a passageway behind this tomb with steps going upwards.

Charlemagne entered the passageway that ran around the side of the tomb and felt that it was humid inside. He started to go upstairs, going around before finally coming to the top. A crawlspace was at Charlemagne's feet. He knelt down and went inside. The vent turned to the right and came into another room – a taller and circular room that was mildly lit with natural light, which seeped in through airways in the roof.

The sunlight fell down upon a casket in the middle of the room. Along the walls of the circular room was a large mural approximately five feet tall that almost wrapped around the entirety of the room. In front of this mural were columns dotted around, seven in total like a heptagon with one on either side from the entrance. Treasure was piled around these columns around almost the entirety of the room, in front of the mural. The sarcophagus in the middle sat atop of a circular platform. Across from the sarcophagus were two columns that led to an enclave with a bust of the same figure from the statues downstairs donning the famed pschent double crown as well as the Amulet of Ra.

"We've found it..." Charlemagne expressed, looking at the dark orb through the pupils of his eyes. "We've actually found it."

Charlemagne stepped forward and came down on one knee to look at the orb. It was as dark as the black diamond he was given. It was also perfectly round and so dark that not a single spec of light reflected from its perfectly smooth surface. It was like a blackhole, wrapped around a light, but strong metal cage, which was like three hoops wrapped around it. The metal of the necklace was brighter than silver and like white gold – scratchless though.

All Charlemagne could do was admire the necklace. He turned off his flashlight and sat down with a pleasant smile. He then turned to the kids who were at the top of the staircase. Charlemagne pointed at the orb.

"This is it," Charlemagne said to them with a smile. "This is the amulet. Diana, get your camera out and take a picture before we disturb it from where it rests."

Charlemagne stood up and got out of the way. Diana looked at him and then opened her backpack to take out the fake necklace, giving it to Tristan and then taking out her camera. She went over to take pictures of the necklace on the bust while Charlemagne looked around with both hands on his hips, admiring the tomb. His eyes looked at a crib as part of the treasures. He looked past this crib and looked at a depiction of a fearful pharaoh on the mural. Charlemagne then turned around to look at the sarcophagus, which was similar to the one below, but shinier and lit by the sunlight above.

"What is this place?" Tristan asked. "Whose tomb is this?"

"I do not know," Charlemagne responded, "but I am looking forward to learning more about it. I'm going to try and decipher as much as I can – Diana, keep taking pictures."

Tristan stuck near Charlemagne as he attempted to translate some of the story. Diana kept taking pictures. Suddenly, the floor shook at their feet. Tristan brushed it off as he frowned.

"Charles, what's your plan for getting us out of here?" Tristan asked, putting the fake necklace into his backpack.

"Not now," Charlemagne replied, "I need to focus on this. It seems like Hatshepsut intended for someone else to rule after her death… perhaps, her daughter? It appears like this tomb was dedicated for her heir, but this heir left her and journeyed elsewhere. Regardless, it is clear by this mural that she did not want Thutmoses III to take over."

Tristan didn't listen. He instead took a step back and went over to Diana who was near the necklace. Tristan crouched down to look at the orb. He stared at it. Diana looked at him as he became lost in it. He shook his head.

"Weird," Tristan remarked, standing up.

"What is it?"

"Whatever that gem is, it did something really weird with my head – it caused my brain to tingle as I looked at it."

"I felt that too when I looked at it. Why do you think that is?"

"It must be something to do with whatever it is," Tristan replied. "Maybe Charles has a better idea."

"Let's make the swap," Diana remarked, stepping towards the necklace. "I've taken enough pictures."

"Sure," Tristan responded, taking the fake back out from his backpack.

Diana picked up the amulet. Diana continued to hold the amulet in her hands. She looked at the orb as it lay in the palm of her hand.

"Diana?" Tristan questioned.

"I don't think this gem is safe to touch," Diana warned, taking the necklace by the chain instead. "What if it's radioactive?"

Tristan frowned as he held the fake. She put the necklace into her backpack. Then, a large explosion knocked them back, pushing them against the wall. Tristan recovered from the blast and looked over to the opposite side of the room where mercenaries dressed in desert camouflage stormed in from the passageway. They had created a hole in the wall to bypass the vent. Tristan then looked to Charlemagne on the ground near them. He produced a revolver from the holster at his belt and fired at the merc.

The bullet went through the shoulder of the mercenary, causing him to drop his rifle and fall to his knees. The mercenaries behind him went forward to subdue Charlemagne.

"No!" Tristan shouted as they took out stun rods and hit Charlemagne on either side.

Another two mercenaries came after the kids, going towards Tristan to take the fake necklace from him. They easily pulled it from his hands before another two went to control them, pressing Tristan's face onto the ground. He looked across the room as he could see Attila enter the room unarmed.

"I want those charges planted here and here," he ordered, pointing at specific areas in the room. "And get them out of here!"

"I have the necklace, sir," the mercenary with the fake necklace said, handing it to Miklos.

Miklos took the necklace and held it by its chain. Tristan and Diana were brought to their feet once their arms were brought behind their back and ties secured their wrists together. Tristan kept his attention on Attila who was looking to Charlemagne.

"Miko!" Charlemagne shouted.

"Get them out!" Miklos shouted. "Move!"

"Yes, sir," a mercenary replied.

Tristan was pushed forward with Diana behind him. Charlemagne was grabbed from the floor and thrown onto the ground again. His arms were then secured behind his back and ties brought around his arms. The kids were led out of the tomb through the hole blown in by the mercs. They were then led out of the false tomb and back into the tunnels where wooden planks had been placed over the gaps in the floor. In addition, wires ran along the walls with a white substance in a plastic wrap stuck onto the walls. Charlemagne was far behind the couple as they were all led out.

Eventually, they were all outside again where it was still afternoon and very warm. A small party of people awaited them near the entrance to the secret tomb. The team composed of Dr. Fischer and Dr. Vidkunsen as well as other associates with the team from Hawara.

Diana and Tristan were brought to them while Charlemagne was pushed onto the ground. Dr. Vidkunsen rushed over to him and dropped to her knees as she saw his wounds.

"Charles, my God!" she complained.

"Bugger off, you hypocrite!" Charlemagne shouted.

"Let him die, doctor," Attila remarked. "Do not waste your time with him."

Tristan glared at Miklos before he then looked over to Charlemagne with concern. Diana also looked, but she was focused on the sound of a helicopter approaching from the east.

"Charles, please," the doctor pleaded as Charlemagne resisted her. "Let me help you."

"Diana... she has the first aid kit," Charlemagne whispered.

Dr. Vidkunsen stood up and went over to Diana. A mercenary raised his weapon and pointed it at her, causing her to raise her hands up.

"Please, let me only take the backpack from the girl," Dr. Vidkunsen reasoned.

The mercenary backed off and allowed her to reach over and take the backpack from her. The merc cut the ties from Diana to get it off, and in that moment, Diana resisted and tried to break free. The mercenary quickly brought her to the ground, causing another two soldiers to run over and assist him re-restrain her.

"Diana!" Tristan shouted, attempting to run towards her.

Another mercenary grabbed him and brought him onto the ground. Both of them met a face full of sand. Dr. Vidkunsen held the backpack tightly around her as she kept her distance.

"Please, not so hard on the children," she pleaded.

The mercenaries ignored her. She went around them to go back to Charlemagne. She opened the backpack and rummaged through. Meanwhile, Tristan looked to Attila and Dr. Fischer as he presented the necklace to the professor.

"*Ist dies das Amulett?*" Attila questioned as the helicopter touched down.

The professor took the necklace and looked at it. He held it with trembling hands, quickly examining it before nodding and returning it to Attila. He continued to hold it by its chain.

"Have these two stripped of their belongings and searched," Attila ordered. "I want them to come with us."

The helicopter was loud. Tristan watched as Diana was brought back onto her feet and made to go towards the helicopter first. Tristan's ties were cut so they could take his backpack from him. They then re-secured the ties around his wrist. He was then brought to his feet and pushed forward. The helicopter door opened to reveal a man in a white suit. Charlemagne squinted at the man as he laid on the ground, being treated by the doctor. He frowned.

"You..." Charlemagne muttered with hate.

"Charlemagne!" Ali al-Suli greeted. "It's been too long! I thought we'd never see each other after what happened in Morocco — it was such a shame to lose you! Ah... you're not looking so good, old friend!"

"We have the necklace as you requested," Attila said, looking at him and then over to Tatiana next to the collector.

"Ah, let me see! Let me see!"

Miklos walked over to them and presented it.

"Oh, it's so ugly and..." Ali responded, weighing it with his hands. "Are you sure this is it?"

"Dr. Fischer confirmed it was the necklace," Miklos replied.

"Bah, what does that doctor know? Ask Charlemagne – Charlemagne, is this the amulet?" Ali asked, showing it to him.

"Go to hell, you son of a bitch!" Charlemagne barked. "I should have known it was you behind all of this!"

The man laughed. He gave the necklace to Tatiana before walking over and squatting near Charlemagne. He took off his sunglasses.

"Do you think it was me who put up the bounty of fifty million? I am flattered, but no. No, it was not me."

"Sir, I've found something," a mercenary spoke in an Eastern European accent.

Tristan watched from the helicopter with Diana. They had found the genuine amulet inside Diana's backpack.

"Ooh, what's this?" Ali remarked, standing up and walking over. "Another amulet?"

"What?" Attila responded. "What is the meaning of this?"

The collector picked up the other necklace and weighed it with his hands.

"Oh, this must be a fake," Ali replied. "It is too light and must be made of tin."

"Which is the real one?" Attila asked Charlemagne, walking over to him.

Charlemagne didn't reply. The doctor continued to treat his wounds. Attila brought his thigh down onto Charlemagne's neck. Charlemagne brought his hands up as he began to be choked.

"Answer me!" Attila demanded.

"Stop! Miko, stop!" Dr. Vidkunsen pleaded, pushing at him. "How can you be so brutal?"

"Do not waste your time, Mr. Horvath," Ali said to Miklos. "Obviously this is the real necklace – the light one is the fake one. Besides, look at this gem – it's obviously made of glass or something."

"Very well," Attila replied, standing up and letting go of Charlemagne.

"However, this gives me an idea," Ali remarked, waving his finger around. "Two necklaces, and I know just the right group who will pay a high price for this necklace."

"The host of the competition?" Miklos questioned.

"No, a higher price!" Ali fiendishly smiled. "Set course for Luxor – we have to meet with the Brethren."

"Yes, sir," Miklos replied, looking over to Tatiana.

"And be sure to destroy any trace of our presence here," Ali added. "We don't need the authorities to know we were here. Hold onto this, Mr. Attila."

Ali threw one of the necklaces to Attila.

"Attila…" Charlemagne muttered. "His name is not Attila."

Attila kicked Charlemagne in the gut.

"Yes, sir," Attila agreed, turning to his men. "Destroy the tomb!"

The mercenaries went forth and triggered the detonator. The ground shook as explosions could be heard.

"*Nein! Nein!*" Dr. Fischer protested, running towards the tomb. "*Warum?*"

"*Halt!*" Miklos shouted, causing mercenaries to run over and grab him.

Ali al-Suli walked over to his helicopter and entered.

"Have Mr. Cabernet join us," Ali requested, waving his hand for them to bring him. "Dr. Fischer and Dr. Vidkunsen as well."

"Here," Miklos said to Gudrun. "I trust you with this – keep it safe."

"Yes, Miko," the doctor replied, taking the necklace before placing it in Diana's backpack.

Charlemagne was picked up by his torso and legs and carried over to the helicopter. Dr. Fischer was dragged towards the helicopter and subdued. Dr. Vidkunsen entered the helicopter carrying Diana's backpack. She boarded the helicopter before Attila did as well.

"Take care of the rest here," Miklos said to Tatiana who did not board. "I will see you soon."

"Of course," she replied.

Tatiana then stepped away as the helicopter began to take off. Ali placed the other necklace he had into a briefcase and then presented it to Attila to hold. He held onto it by his hand from where he stood.

Act 5, Scene 1

The helicopter made a short trip from the Temple of Queen Hatshepsut and into Luxor – a large modern town in Upper Egypt. The sky had gone grey with clouds in that time, but the air was still humid and warm if not warmer. Dr. Vidkunsen had finished patching up Charlemagne with bandages and he was now sitting on the ground. The doctor sat across from him with Diana's backpack on her lap. Ali al-Suli did not sit in the back of the helicopter, but instead sat at the front with the pilot. Attila continued to stand throughout the entire ride and was accompanied by one other mercenary. Diana and Tristan also sat on the floor, next to Charlemagne. Dr. Fischer was asleep on the floor across from the kids. Nobody talked during the entire ride.

The helicopter made its descent into a large pavilion outside a large temple made of pillars of sandstone. It was in the middle of the city on the bank of the Nile pier and was lit by bright construction light towers. Two large statues of Egyptian figures stood guard at the entrance with high walls behind them.

The doors of the helicopter were opened by two local men wearing dark green uniforms with the Egyptian Republic flag on either side and red berets over their head. Attila stepped forward with the briefcase. The mercenary in the back of the helicopter raised his gun out for the kids to move. Ali exited the plan and spoke in Arabic to the other soldiers. One of them began to drag Dr. Fischer out and onto the ground. Dr. Vidkunsen stood up with Diana's back and also picked up Tristan's. The other mercenary took Charlemagne's, which was handed to Attila. Dr. Fischer began to wake up.

"*Steh auf, Doktor,*" Miklos ordered. "*Zeigen Sie etwas Integritat.*"

"*Ja...*" Dr. Fischer replied, following them as they all walked forward.

All of them followed the Egyptian soldiers towards the entrance of the Karnak Temple where more of them stood guard. The collector saluted the men with a foolish smile. He spoke in Arabic, pointed to the trio, and then over to Attila with the briefcase. The guards looked at him with a serious face. One of them picked up a radio and spoke in Arabic through it. He waited for a response, which came shortly after. They then waited again, and another transmission came.

Ali al-Suli was permitted through and the others followed from behind They walked down a tall corridor to reach a center where thick cylindrical pillars surrounded them on one side and a sandstone building or annex on the other. The interior had more construction light towers creating a bright atmosphere in the complex. There were also a lot of crates, munition crates, and tall screens behind the pillars. Ahead of them was an entrance to another corridor with more pillars and only screens behind them. The men inside this sector wore balaclavas and different uniforms. They were armed with Kalashnikovs and looked onto the party as they travelled to the opposite end. They were stopped there and then escorted deeper into the open section, or courtyard, which was also surrounded by pillars at the perimeter.

Some men could be seen on ladders, tying white packets of explosives around. They left this area and entered the actual temple, following the wires and explosives into a section which was not roofed, but did have walls with engravings, writings and other ancient art. Finally, the group came to the end of the temple where they found a single man sitting on a throne. He was dressed much the same as the others: balaclava and tactical vest, but he wore a red-white checkered scarf around his neck and was unarmed like Attila. He had his arms spread on the rests of the throne. In front of him was a TV camera pointed towards his throne. Between the camera and throne was a pit with wooden furniture inside. Towards the side of the throne was a black flag with Arabic text atop.

One of the guards spoke in Arabic to him. He raised his hands up and signaled the collector to step forward. Ali stepped forward, turning around to face the group as he extended a hand towards the man on the throne.

"May I introduce to you, my dear friends, the Khan of the Brethren of Islam in Egypt!"

The billionaire then turned back to the Khan on his throne with his smug face.

"Do you have it? The necklace that all of them are taking about?" the Khan questioned in a coarse British accent.

"I do," Ali replied with a shrewd smile.

"Give it to me," the Khan demanded.

Ali turned around and had Attila step forward with the briefcase. Attila walked over to Ali and gave the briefcase to him. Ali then turned around and opened it to show the Khan.

The Khan stood up and stepped forward. He stepped down to Ali and took the necklace from the briefcase, examining it before setting it back inside the briefcase.

"It is the one and true Amulet of Ra that you requested, sir," Ali explained. "All yours for a handsome price."

"I see nothing special about this... it is nothing more than a relic of the pagans and should be destroyed."

Ali went quiet and nodded. He closed the briefcase and handed it to the Khan.

"I'll accept my payment at once then," al-Suli boasted.

Charlemagne frowned as he watched this. He then cleared his throat and straightened his posture.

"It's fake," Charlemagne stated.

"What?" the Khan questioned as Ali cringed.

"The real necklace is in that backpack over there," Charlemagne said in a calm tone, pointing to Diana's backpack with his head. "The one you have is fake – Mr. Suli was attempting to swindle you."

"Is this true?" the Khan questioned Ali, who took a step backwards.

"No, it is not – this man speaks lies to you," Ali argued. "Look at him. Who is he? He is a dirty Westerner and enemy of our people!"

"Prove it! Show me the backpack!"

Ali looked over to Attila who held a hand at his belt, close to a holster around his thigh. A terrorist goon walked over to Dr. Vidkunsen and snatched the backpacks from her hands. The goon then opened each of them, taking out the other necklace and showing it to everyone in the room. The terrorist leader saw and then glared at Ali who took another step back.

"No, no! That is the fake – I swear! I intended to sell you the true amulet!" Ali reasoned.

"You insolent fool!" the Khan shouted, raising a hand to strike the billionaire.

The Khan hesitated and lowered his hand.

"If it weren't for your usefulness still, I'd have you slain at once! Do you not realize that we require the *true* amulet in order to fulfill our vision? Of a truly Islamic Egypt?"

Ali gave a sigh of relief and stepped backwards.

"Yes, well, I'll tell you what," Ali said with a nervous laugh, "you can keep both of the necklaces and I'll take that payment later."

"Leave us!" the Khan shouted at him.

Ali rushed towards the exit. Miklos stepped towards him to follow him. Dr. Vidkunsen attempted to leave too alongside Dr. Fischer.

"Leave these witnesses!" the Khan shouted. "They have seen too much. They will all be executed to send a message of strength."

"Yes, yes," Ali replied, waving towards them. "Have them – I'm done here!"

Ali then left the room and ran away. Miklos drew his pistol out, but refrained from firing it as terrorists drew assault rifles on him. He simply dropped the gun and brought his hands up. They then went over and forced him onto his knees.

A terrorist brought the other necklace to the Khan. The Khan took it into his hands, looked at it and then gave it back to the goon. He also gave him the briefcase. The Khan spoke in Arabic, taking out a machete and pointing for the subordinate to take the items away. The goon went back to the others, fetching Tristan's backpack and Charlemagne's backpack. Another goon collected Miklos' pistol on the ground and disarmed him of other weapons as well as the mercenary in the back of the room who was brought closer to the group. Tristan watched as all these items were placed on a table in the back of the room, on the right-side of the exit near a corner where there was a pillar. In front of the pillar was a pile of broken wooden furniture. Next to this pile was a table where the items were being left. The backpacks were placed on the left of the table, the briefcase on the right, and the other necklace between the briefcase and the backpack. Dr. Vidkunsen was also forced onto her knees with her hands placed above her head.

"Have the girl taken away for later," the Khan ordered. "For the crimes of their nations, they will pay with their blood! Start the camera!"

Diana was pulled from the crowd.

"Hey, let go of me!" she cried out.

"Diana!" Tristan objected, turning to go towards her.

"Tristan!" Charlemagne scolded, looking over to terrorists who had raised their assault rifles towards him.

Tristan turned to him and then looked to the terrorists. He then turned back to the front.

"They're going to take Diana away," Tristan told Charlemagne. "I won't let anything happen to her!"

"All of Egypt will be torn from their pagan symbols – a purification for a New Egypt!" the Khan boasted. "From today onwards, a new revolution will ignite!"

A terrorist goon poured gasoline onto the firepit and then threw a match, lighting the bonfire in front of the camera. The Khan stood behind the fire and took out a pistol to hold in his other hand.

"Bring him to me," the leader requested, pointing to Dr. Fischer.

"*Nein,*" Dr. Fischer rejected, shaking his head.

Two terrorists took the professor by either arm and then dragged him to the terrorist leader. His wrists were tied behind his back with rope and he was made to go down on his knees. The terrorist leader spoke in Arabic around the room. Tristan's eyes could not keep up with all the activity. A terrorist took charge of the camera pointed at the professor and Khan.

"*Bitte, ich habe nichts getan!*" Dr. Fischer cried out.

"Let him go!" Charlemagne demanded. "He's innocent!"

"Silence!" the terrorist leader said. "You will be next!"

Diana was taken away from the throne room and brought to a separate room where she was thrown inside. The two terrorists that had escorted her to the damp, dark room looked at her and then closed the door behind her.

The Khan spoke in Arabic to the camera. He brought his machete and placed it underneath the chin of Dr. Fischer. The light of the fire revealed the nervous sweat atop of the professor's face. The Khan then removed the machete and pointed it to the camera. He raised the machete up with a shout.

"*Allahu akbar!*" the Khan proclaimed.

The Khan then tilted the professor's head back, bringing the blade to his neck and then slicing the flesh. Blood poured out. The professor screamed.

Tristan immediately closed his eyes upon the sight of blood. However, he could not refrain from hearing the screams and gurgling of blood. He tried to move his face to the side, but it made no difference. In less than a minute, the screams stopped and he could bring his face forward again, opening his eyes with hesitance to look forward in horror.

The professor had been beheaded. Two terrorists walked forward to pick up the beheaded body and throw it into the pit. Tristan panted as he saw all this. He then looked behind him and began to struggle in his ties. Suddenly, gunshots were heard from above.

Charlemagne and Tristan ducked as they heard the gunfire. The terrorists responded and opened fire. Charlemagne kept his head down but looked over to Miklos who with his hands still tied behind his back, began to engage with the terrorist nearby. Charlemagne's hands were freed all of the sudden. He looked behind him and saw Dr. Vidkunsen with a knife in her hand. She then ran over to free Tristan.

"I'll grab the necklace," Charlemagne told Tristan.

"We need to rescue Diana!" Tristan replied.

Charlemagne ran over to the table. Tristan watched as Miklos saw this after taking down the guard watching him.

"Charles, look out!" Tristan shouted.

Charlemagne grabbed the necklace in the middle and then turned to see Miklos charging towards him. Behind the room, rope had been thrown down against the wall with mercenaries in desert camouflage rappelling down. They engaged the terrorists who had been backed to the other side of the room.

"Tristan!" Charlemagne shouted, tossing the necklace towards him.

Tristan caught it just as his hands were freed. He was then forced to duck was Dr. Vidkunsen brought him onto the ground with gunshots flying over them.

"Run!" Charlemagne remarked as he went to the exit.

Attila tackled Charlemagne onto the ground before he could exit. Tristan came up and looked over as he saw a familiar female figure running towards him. He then stood up and ran towards his things. Tatiana grabbed him before he could get his backpack. Tristan squirmed and threw the necklace forward, behind the pile of furniture.

In Tatiana's distraction, he elbowed her in the stomach, causing her to let go of him. He then walked forward and grabbed a piece of wood to lunge at her with. The mercenary dodged out of the way. Tristan lunged at her again. She grabbed the piece of wood and threw it away. She then grabbed him and brought him onto the floor.

"Stay down, child," Tatiana warned. "The scope of all of this is beyond you."

The temple began to vibrate with the sound of explosions. Charlemagne watched as a packet of explosives detonated at the bases of pillars around the room, causing them to tumble over. Tatiana grabbed Tristan and pushed him out of the way before she rolled out of the opposite way. Likewise, a pillar collapsed between him and Miklos.

Tristan covered his eyes from the dust. The floor continued to tremor. He ran over to the table and took his backpack, leaving Charlemagne's behind. Tristan looked at Charlemagne's backpack before looking over to the exit where he saw Dr. Vidkunsen leaving with Diana's backpack. He then looked at the empty briefcase before seeing the necklace on the ground. He picked it up and then went around to the exit where he met Charlemagne.

"Come on, let's rescue Diana and leave," Charlemagne stated.

"Agreed."

• •

Diana sat against the wall in her damp cell with her arms still tied behind her back. She then looked up as she saw a figure approaching through the window in the door. The door opened to reveal a terrorist, unmasked and unarmed. He entered the room and then closed the door behind him. Diana stared back at him with focused eyes. The man began to sing in Arabic as he unloaded all sorts of equipment from his belt before taking it off and placing it on the table next to the door. The man then walked towards Diana and squatted down next to her. He spoke in Arabic to her, bringing a hand to her face. Diana raised her leg to kick him. The terrorist swatted her leg.

The terrorist raised a fist to her. She spat in his face and then headbutted him. She then tried to get up, but the terrorist, screaming at her, stood up and grabbed her by the arm. Diana proceeded to kick him. The terrorist threw her onto the wall and proceeded to bring his hands onto her body while holding her against the wall. The terrorist produced a knife, which Diana could see with frightened eyes. Diana quickly turned her body, kicking the terrorist in the chin and causing him to go backwards. She then ran to the table, grabbed the first item she could spot (a knife) and threw it at the terrorist, piercing his shoulder.

The room vibrated and the sound of an explosion could be heard. Diana quickly ran to the door, opened it and fled. She ran down the corridor she was brought along. At the junction, she ran into someone, causing her to step back in fear. Diana calmed down though as she saw that it was Dr. Vidkunsen with her backpack.

"Diana, thank goodness," Dr. Vidkunsen said. "Here, my dear. Let me set you free."

The doctor produced a knife. Diana took a step back.

"Turn around, quickly."

Diana turned around and felt her hands become free as the ties were cut. She then turned back around as the doctor put the knife away. She handed Diana her backpack. Diana took it. The doctor then placed a hand on Diana's shoulder.

"Are you alright, my dear?" the doctor asked.

"I'm... I've been better," Diana confessed, "but what's going on? Where are the others?"

Diana turned to the side as she saw Tristan and Charlemagne running towards them. Charlemagne stopped before them. Tristan went forward and hugged Diana.

"Oh, Diana, thank God!" Charlemagne remarked.

Tristan parted from Diana; the couple then looked at the adults.

"You must leave at once," the doctor told them. "Go."

"Agreed, but what about you?" Charlemagne questioned.

"I will be safe," the doctor replied. "I am with Miklos."

"You helped us," Tristan said to her.

"And I would appreciate it if that help were not in vain – go!" the doctor insisted.

"Thank you, doctor," Charlemagne replied before looking to the kids. "You heard her, let's go!"

Charlemagne and them ran and came to the courtyard. Some more explosions could be heard, causing the exit on the opposite side to collapse into two. Charlemagne looked around before pointing to an exit.

"Here!" Charlemagne shouted to the kids, rushing to the right so they could escape.

The group ran underneath some pillars that had tiled and left the temple, but not the property as they were about to face a chain-link fence past some tall grass on the outskirts. The three of them climbed over and started to run just as the rest of the temple detonated into a large explosion. The warmth of the fireball fell upon them as they dropped to the ground on the other side.

Diana looked over and saw some more mercenaries stationed around the perimeter of the temple. Tristan grabbed her wrist and the couple stood up. The two of them followed Charlemagne down the street and towards some stopped traffic where onlookers had exited their vehicle to observe the horror, grabbing it with their smartphones.

Charlemagne ran to a vacant van where the drive behind was filming the travesty. He opened the door and ushered the kids in before entering and taking control of the steering wheel. He changed the gears of the van before he drove off, causing the owner of the van to shout and curse.

"Sorry…" Charlemagne muttered.

The van drove off and away from the temple. Sirens could be heard in the distance. He looked in the side-view mirror to see smoke rising up from the temple into the air with flashing sirens behind them, turning onto the edge of the property. He slowed down his speed and drove normally as he drove back to their hotel.

Tristan calmed down as he sat in the back of the van. He looked at the necklace and began to hold it by its chain, looking at the orb. With alert, he looked at the orb and took both hands to hold the chain.

"No... no!" Tristan complained. "I have the wrong necklace!"

"What?" Charlemagne questioned, looking into the rear-view mirror.

"I have the wrong necklace!" he repeated. "I can tell – this one is heavier and isn't giving me the same effect."

Charlemagne didn't reply. He continued to drive and pulled onto the curb outside of the hotel. He then turned around and looked over. Tristan brought him the necklace. He took it into his hands and looked.

"Impossible," Charlemagne remarked. "I was sure to grab the true amulet – how could I have been mistaken?"

Diana looked at both of them and then looked to the side.

"What are we going to do then?" Diana asked in a quiet voice.

Charlemagne sighed.

"I'm not sure – but we can think about this on the road back to Cairo. We cannot stay here. We need to take our things from our room and leave."

Act 5, Scene 2

After leaving their hotel, Charlemagne drove into the night from Luxor, stopping at a motel half-way to Cairo. The next morning, they continued their trip and made it into Giza. For both segments of their trip, they were quiet and held saddened faces. It did not help that the skies were grey. Charlemagne drove the stolen van into Giza, parked it on the side of a road near the same hotel they had checked in to at the start of the trip.

Charlemagne looked into the back of the truck where the kids were sleeping. He looked at both of them with saddened faces and raised a smile.

"Children..." Charlemagne said to them.

Diana flinched and woke up, which caused Tristan to wake up.

"We're here," Charlemagne explained. "Come, we have a short walk back to the hotel where you can rest on a proper bed."

Charlemagne and the couple exited the van and they went into the hotel lobby before going to their floor.

"The entire country is in a state of emergency," Charlemagne remarked once they were in the elevator.

The elevator doors opened on their floor and Charlemagne stepped forward to open the door. He took out his card key and inserted it.

"I'm going to give the Canadian embassy a call to see if I can send you there," Charlemagne explained as he attempted to unlock the door. "I'll continue on my own."

"Hell no," Diana rejected.

"No ifs," Charlemagne remarked. "You have been put through enough danger as it is – what occurred in Luxor was over the top for either of you, and I will not be left with guilt should something happen to either of you."

Charlemagne opened the door and entered.

"Stop!" a voice shouted from within.

Charlemagne jumped and looked forward. He then lowered his expression as he closed his eyes in relief.

"Oh, Johnathan, put that down," Charlemagne remarked.

"It's you," Johnathan said with relief, setting down a coat rack. "I thought you were dead or arrested. Where the hell have you been?"

"It's a long story, but I take it you've heard the news about Luxor."

"No, why?"

"Well, it was blown up last night alongside the subbasement of the Temple of Queen Hatshepsut," Charlemagne said, grabbing a TV remote and turning it on.

"What? Why? How?"

"Well, the latter was blown by competitors and the former by religious extremists," Charlemagne explained, sitting down at the couch. "I have lots to tell you since we last saw each other in Hawara."

Diana left to grab a shower. Tristan sat down on a kitchen chair. Charlemagne proceeded to explain the last three days since Hawara from the kidnapping, being left in the Sinai Desert, finding shelter at a monastery, exploring a tomb in the Temple of Queen Hatshepsut, and finally witnessing horrors at the Luxor Temple. He also explained the role of Ali al-Suli as the one that hired Dr. Fischer as well as the mercenaries and Doctor Vidkunsen. He then explained the unfortunate conclusion of Dr. Fischer at the hands of a terrorist.

Tristan looked at the ground in silence. He shook his head and then looked over to the adults.

"My God," Johnathan reacted, taking a deep breath. "I'm not surprised it was that same shill from Morocco."

"Right… and he's still at large and we don't have the necklace. Either these Jihadis or mercenaries have it, and neither of them are good people. We need to move forward with expectation that the worst is true. Imagine what these savages might do with the power of that necklace in their hands. The patriarch told me that even if whoever has the orb is not gifted, one can still harness powers from that orb that are unmatched."

"So, what do you want us to do? To fight terrorism?" Johnathan questioned with slight sarcasm.

"No, but we need to find the other orb. We need to secure it before it gets into the hands of these fiends as well. Who knows what they would be able to achieve if they had both in their hands!" Charlemagne said. "We'll need it if we intend to defeat these foes."

"Wait, what?" Johnathan questioned. "Are you serious? I thought we were just here to collect the Amulet of Ra – not to fight extremists or collect magical orbs."

"We are here for the orbs and only the orbs, and we need to get that other orb back!" Charlemagne insisted. "I need – I need to do some research and learn where this other orb is. My old notes said that Ramses II had collected it, but we need to know where it went from there."

Diana returned from her shower, dressed in clean clothing. She then went over to Tristan and stood behind him.

"You can go for a shower now if you want," she said to him.

Tristan nodded to her and stood up. She sat down where he was sitting.

"I need to go to the Cairo University and get as many books as possible," Charlemagne explained. "We need to know where that orb went, understood?"

"Yes, sir," Johnathan replied.

Johnathan stood up from the couch and left to get his things. He then returned to leave through the front door. Before he could, his attention diverted out the window and towards the pyramids as they heard a loud boom. The room vibrated. Charlemagne turned around and looked out the window. He stood up and got a closer look. Johnathan simply looked from where he was as smoke rose from the pyramids. Sirens could be heard in the background.

"No... they've hit the pyramids," Charlemagne expressed before turning to Johnathan. "We need to hurry."

Johnathan nodded and left. Tristan entered the room and went to look out the window, still dressed in his original clothes. He then entered the living room where the others were.

"What's going on?" Tristan asked.

Charlemagne went back around to the couch and picked up the remote. He turned on the TV and flipped to a news channel. Meanwhile, Diana stood up and fetched her backpack. She opened it and quickly retrieved her camera, taking it and going over to take pictures. Charlemagne found some Arabic news channels but could not understand anything. He then found the BBC and watched.

"... Egyptian authorities are responding, but we have yet to be informed of damage and possible casualties," a spokeswoman said. "Again, the blast seems to have occurred at the Giza pyramids and initial observations show that the Great Pyramid and Great Sphinx were hit in the blast. We are unsure of the origin of the blast so far."

Charlemagne muted the TV and laid back in his seat. Diana turned around as she saw Tristan enter their room.

"Hey, can I use your laptop?" she asked.

"Sure, why?"

"There's something I want to look at," she replied.

Tristan nodded and then went to take his shower.

• •

Later that evening, Charlemagne and Johnathan sat around a pile of work and books at the kitchen table while Diana used Tristan's computer and Tristan attempted to get some rest in the bedroom with earphones in his ears.

"I simply do not understand where this orb could be..." Charlemagne complained. "At best, we've confirmed the Kushites never got their hands on the orb..."

"We can rule out the Turks and Arabs," Johnathan added. "There are no historical accounts from either of these groups."

"The Byzantines and Romans can be ruled out too. I'm sure the patriarch would have said something had he known about the second orb – he was of the opinion that it was lost too."

"So, that brings us to the Ptolemaic period, but we have nothing from them either," Johnathan complained.

"Yes, the Greeks, like the Romans, were very thorough with their records and I do not see anything here about an orb in Luxor."

"Before the Greeks, it was the Persians, but unlike the Romans and Greeks, they were miserable at keeping records."

"Hey, Charles," Diana interrupted.

"What is it, Diana?" Charlemagne asked, looking over and removing his reading glasses.

"I was doing some of my own research about something that might help us," Diana replied. "Do you remember those mercenaries that 'helped' us in Russia?"

"Help is a loose term for what they did, but yes, I do remember them."

"I've been doing some digging about them, and I think I have a connection between them and your friend, Mr. Zimmerman."

"What connection?" Charlemagne asked, looking at the computer screen.

"Well, according to some news articles, apparently they do a lot of work for Mr. Zimmerman's company, Zimmerman Corps. I was interested in this because at the start of the competition, I learned that they were providing security for this competition and I've been starting to think about possible people who could be hosting this competition."

"Where did you learn that they were providing security for this competition?" Charlemagne questioned.

"Johnathan told me when he met them to tool us up last week," Diana replied.

"You got help from those mercenaries?" Charlemagne queried, looking to Johnathan who froze up.

"Well, I… yeah. You told me to get supplies, and Zimmerman recommended me to go to them."

"So, is Zimmerman behind this race?" Diana asked. "He's the reason you're here, Charles. It would only make sense why he'd force you in if he wanted you to find it for himself."

Charlemagne looked at her and then down at the table. He didn't reply.

"I can't believe it to be true. Audric wouldn't use me like that. He isn't using me. He never offered me money – he knows that's not good enough and he knows that if I were to find the orbs, I would never hand them to him. I could not believe he's behind this."

"Who says you would have to hand them to him. For all we know, these mercenaries stole your laptop on purpose and he hired Sergei Bykov for the benefit of himself. He could easily intimidate you into giving the orbs."

"Enough, Diana," Charlemagne protested in anger. "Zimmerman is not our enemy. I doubt Audric is working against us. The contest is of no matter right now – we need to focus on the second orb and get that necklace back."

"How about Siwa?" Johnathan said to change the topic back to the orb.

"Sorry?" Charlemagne replied.

"It's the only place we could search, Charles. According to some Greek records, when the Persians invaded, the Egyptian priests moved a load of artefacts to Siwa in anticipating for their next rule. Of course, no native rulers came about, but there was one person that the Egyptians revered as their savior and might have gifted the orb in return for liberating them."

"Alexander the Great?" Charlemagne replied, "but no one has found his tomb."

"Not exactly, and the timing of all this is perfect because a professor of mine boasted that he knew of the tomb's location, but due to Macedonian nationalism and internal strife with the Egyptian government, the area was blocked off to prevent archeologists from investigating it. The place is in Siwa, which coincidentally is where Alexander wanted to be interred. I believe it's our best shot for finding this orb."

"Siwa… Alexander…" Charlemagne muttered, looking at the map. "It's far from us and it's a small town, but I have no clue how we might secure transport over there… not to mention protection from all those that seek to destroy us."

"Let me talk to the Huntsman then," Johnathan offered. "I'm sure we can come to some sort of arrangement with them if we let them know we might have the possible location of the necklace – or bribe them with the fake one we have."

"Are we still going to have to go to Canada?" Tristan asked, listening in on the conversation the whole time as he stood under the door frame of his bedroom. "If Siwa is far and we're going to be protected, won't it be safe enough for us to come along?"

Charlemagne sighed and looked at him.

"Tristan, you know as well as I know that I have a duty and responsibility to protect you as a guardian. I cannot let you keep getting into harm's way."

"Like you almost let us get hurt in Russia?" Diana questioned. "We survived then and we'll survive now. We're not kids, Charles. I'm turning sixteen in August and Tristan's going to be sixteen in November. We know how to handle ourselves and I'm not going to let you treat us like kids and take us out of the fight just like that. We can handle it. Let us come. We won't get in the way."

Charlemagne sighed. Johnathan didn't say anything and simply looked down in awkwardness of the conversation.

"It could be a learning experience," Tristan added. "I mean, what if one of us decided to continue this in the future? Better now than later, right?"

"Fine! Fine, you can come, but only because this is Siwa and not Luxor or even Cairo. I'm sure we will be safe and far from the others but understand that as soon as we get this orb, that's when I draw the line and send you home. Am I clear?"

"Yes, sir," Diana replied with a smile.

Act 5, Scene 3

Diana and Tristan sat across from Johnathan and Charlemagne aboard a Mi-26 helicopter piloted by Huntsman mercenaries. They were escorted by three others in bullet proof vests. Charlemagne said little to any of them.

The helicopter started its descent into the restricted area and Charlemagne looked out the window to see a hill with a simple hut over what appeared to be entrance to the tomb. The site was deserted. The hill the tomb seemed to have been built on was tall, clean-cut and narrow. The helicopter doors opened and Charlemagne was let out with Diana, Tristan and Johnathan.

"We need to refuel the helicopter," the mercenary said to Charlemagne. "Call us when are ready to leave."

"We will" Johnathan replied for him, waving them goodbye.

The helicopter lifted up into the air and went off. Once it was far away, all that was left was the silence atop of the hill they were on. It was also warm and windy. The hill looked down onto the town of Siwa.

"Well, let's get going," Charlemagne said.

Charlemagne stepped forward and looked at the entrance of the tomb. He looked at the Doric pillars and the lion statues on either side of the tomb entrance. He took out his flashlight, turned it on, and placed it in his lapel pocket. He then walked forward to approach the boards that covered the tomb entrance.

"Help me kick this down," Charlemagne said to Johnathan.

The two of them kicked it down, revealing a cave-like corridor with chiseled sandstone floor. Charlemagne led the way forward into the long tunnel before they met the end, which split into two paths on each side.

"Tristan, stay with Johnathan. Diana, stay with me. We'll split up and see where this takes us," Charlemagne ordered.

Nobody argued against him. Charlemagne went up the long steps of the cave until they reached a connection between the opposite stairs and came together with the others. The stairs continued together and upwards, much as they did in the Great Pyramid. At the end, the exit was blocked by more wooden planks.

Johnathan kicked the wood down, revealing sunlight that poured in. Several more steps followed to lead them out of the trench and onto the top of the previous mound. All of them exited the entrance way and stood atop the plateau of a large rock. It had similar chiseled-style to the reddish rocks of this area of Egypt and it wrapped around and had a smooth top.

Upwards, there was scaffolding and some yellow tape that blocked the trail, which split into two directions that wrapped around. Some parts of the trail were cut-off from each other, and in general, the entire pathway looked dangerous to climb with risks of rockfall. Charlemagne could see a man-made tunnel up above going into the hill. The hill itself was more like a natural pyramid that reached upwards to the sky. Charlemagne shielded his eyes from the sun and looked back down from where they first inserted. They were about twenty feet up, which was in addition to the fact that they were already at a high altitude.

"So, we climb that?" Tristan asked.

"Yes," Charlemagne replied.

Each of them paused for a moment as they began to hear the rotos of a helicopter approaching.

"They can't be back so soon…" Charlemagne whispered.

"Perhaps they've sent us reinforcements for protection?" Johnathan questioned.

Charlemagne took out the revolver he had holstered and Johnathan did the same. They eyed the helicopter in the distance and could see it was a different model – a Chinook.

"They didn't say they were bringing reinforcements…" Charlemagne replied.

"What are we going to do?" Tristan questioned.

"We're going to wait here to see who they are," Charlemagne explained. "However, I want you and Diana to take the right path and go ahead. Do not come down until we say it is safe to do so, understood?"

"Yes, sir," Tristan replied, taking Diana's hand. "Let's go."

Diana nodded and the two of them rushed off towards the entrance, ducking under the yellow tape to get through.

"These aren't Huntsmen," Charlemagne noted, loading his revolver. "These are Attila's men. I'll take the right side; you take the left side. We'll hold them back until our men can get back from the airfield."

"Yes, Mr. Cabernet," Johnathan replied as Charlemagne span the cylinder of his revolver.

"Be careful, son."

"I will, Mr. Cabernet."

Johnathan left and went around to the opposite side of the plateau. Charlemagne went to the edge of his side and knelt down. The helicopter made its approach close enough for Charlemagne to recognize and confirm that Attila was here for them. The copter started to hover down near where Charlemagne and the kids were dropped off.

Diana and Tristan had paused not too far from the trail to look over to Charlemagne and Johnathan getting ready for a gunfight. Diana watched for another second before she tugged at Tristan's wrist so they could keep going together.

"We don't need to see this, we need to keep going," she said.

"Right…" Tristan replied.

The two of them went forward to a ladder. Diana went up first followed by Tristan. The couple arrived onto the second level.

Charlemagne watched as the doors of the helicopter opened to reveal two mercenaries getting out. Charlemagne took the first shot, hitting one in the shoulder and sending him back. The other panicked and started to fire upwards, towards Charlemagne. He ducked, giving Johnathan opportunity to take out the other. Attila and Tatiana left the helicopter next, firing their guns and forcing Charlemagne to hide behind a rock.

"Charlemagne, you've brought a lot more fight with you this time," Attila shouted. "We will take that necklace off you by your dead body!"

"Stand down, Miklos! The terrorists have the necklace – not us! You're letting them get away with this!" Charlemagne shouted. "You're working for a man who sold you out! Al-Suli will surely do it again!"

"I don't care who ends up with that necklace, Charles!" Attila replied. "I only intend on getting paid!"

Charlemagne peaked from around the rock and saw Gudrun, Francisco, and Benito exit from the helicopter and rush towards the entrance unarmed. He moved to fire at Attila again, but he returned fire with a rifle, grazing Charlemagne's arm.

"Damn…" Charlemagne complained, bringing a hand to his wound. "Johnathan, they're coming up – get ready to ambush them!"

"Will do!"

"Tatiana, escort them," Attila ordered. "I'll take care of the old man and keep the landing zone clear."

Charlemagne peaked around the corner to notice Attila give his wife a kiss on the cheek before she set off.

"I'm disappointed in you, Tatia," Charlemagne shouted. "You were never one to help monsters!"

"Do not listen to him. Get to the others!" Attila replied.

The helicopter started to lift up before it departed. Charlemagne reloaded his revolver before looking around. Some more gunfire came from Attila as he continued to pin Charlemagne down at his current location. He saw Johnathan get to the trench by the entrance where more gunfire was coming out of.

"Charles, it's too hot. She's giving them too much covering fire for me to do much," Johnathan said.

"Hold your position!" Charlemagne ordered.

Diana and Tristan made their way around the second level, coming to the third where the paths were narrower. They continued and looked down at where the action was happening.

"Don't look down," Tristan said, grabbing Diana's wrist. "You know you're afraid of heights."

"Sorry," Diana replied, looking away.

"Let's keep going…"

Tristan took a step to the side onto some unstable ground, causing him to fall. Diana grabbed him by the straps of his backpack.

"Tristan!" Diana shouted.

Charlemagne looked up and saw what was happening with fearful eyes.

"Good God," Charlemagne muttered. "Johnathan, my children! Abandon your post – go help them!"

Johnathan didn't hesitate to abandon his position and run off. Charlemagne looked over to Francisco and Benito coming out from the entrance. Charlemagne fired towards them, causing them to duck before splitting up. Dr. Vidkunsen came through next. Charlemagne fired towards her as well, causing her to drop down in fear.

"I don't want to hurt any of you!" Charlemagne shouted.

"Please, Charles, I am not your enemy," she said, bringing her hands behind her neck. "You don't understand!"

"I understand perfectly well!" Charlemagne yelled, looking up as he saw Diana struggling to keep Tristan up.

Johnathan arrived and pulled them both to safety.

"Careful," Tristan said, panting. "The ground is unsteady."

"Noted," Johnathan replied, looking back at them before looking down. "Keep moving – I've got your backs."

Johnathan fired down at Attila, causing him to take cover as he was suppressing Charlemagne.

"You're wounded," Dr. Vidkunsen said, looking over to Charlemagne. "Let me help you."

Charlemagne looked at her and decided to raise his gun so he could go over and over the doorway now that Attila had stopped suppressing him. She took out a medikit and set it down when Tatiana arrived. Charlemagne immediately grabbed the doctor by the neck and used her as a human shield. Tatiana kept her assault rifle aimed at them.

"Stand down or I will fire," Charlemagne threatened.

"Please, let me go," Dr. Vidkunsen pleaded.

"Charles…" Tatiana said in her elegant accent. "You and I both know that you won't hurt Guda."

The two of them started to take side-steps as they span around each other.

"I wouldn't be so sure – you were nearly responsible for the deaths of my children when you abandoned us," Charlemagne stated.

"I gave you water, and I knew you weren't far from that monastery," she argued as they continued to side-step.

"It took us the entire day to walk there!"

Johnathan shot down at Tatiana, missing her and causing her to jump back as she looked up.

"Shoot her if you want, Charles, but I'm gone," she said, running off and towards the left pathway.

"Damn," Charlemagne remarked, letting go of Gudrun.

"Mr. Cabernet, Attila the Hun is coming your way – prepare yourself!" Johnathan warned.

"Understood, son! I'm coming to you know – keep my children safe!" Charlemagne replied, taking out some plastic ties to subdue the doctor. "You stay right here, my dear. I need no more trouble from you."

Charlemagne then left and went up the left-side of the trail. Tristan and Diana dodged the unstable ground at their feet and came to the level above Johnathan where he was providing overwatch. Tristan noticed Francisco making his approach.

"Johnny, on your right! Watch out!" Tristan yelled.

Johnathan sprang to life and aimed his gun over to the old Spaniard, firing a shot past him and causing him to tackle him. The two of them fought, but Johnathan overcame him and punched him in the face.

"That's for betraying us in Abydos," Johnathan remarked, taking him down to tie him up.

Tristan watched for another second before he noticed Attila exit the entrance. He took Diana by the wrist and they continued.

Charlemagne continued along the left trail until he was tackled by Benito. The two of them slid down to the second level. Charlemagne's revolver had fallen from his grip and landed between them. They both launched for it, but Charlemagne had beaten him to it and still tackled Benito onto the ground. Charlemagne kept his grip tight around the grip of the handgun, and when he could, he could hit Benito in the face with the blunt weapon.

Benito fell backwards with a bloodied nose, letting Charlemagne stand up and thrown him onto his back to tie him down. He then took a deep breath and continued upwards.

Diana and Tristan continued along the fourth level of the trail before they reached an extremely narrow ledge for them to shuffle across. Tristan kept Diana's hand in his as they crossed before continuing along to the fifth level. Tristan stopped again as he noticed Tatiana beneath them on a different trail two levels down. He looked above him to see how far they had left. He then let go of Diana's hand, causing her to look at him.

"We should split up," Tristan suggested. "I can slow down the girl while you go to the top."

"When we get up there, what exactly is our plan to escape?" Diana asked him.

"Slide down?" Tristan replied with a light smile. "Be careful, okay? We're going to get through this in one piece."

Diana looked at Tristan with a worried smile. Tristan kissed her on the cheek before he came to the edge of the cliff and slid down to intercept Tatiana. Diana looked down for a split second before continuing along and onwards.

Tristan looked forward in the next minute. Tatiana showed up and raised her weapon at him. Tristan raised his hands up.

"I'm just a kid, you know," Tristan said. "You wouldn't shoot a kid, would you? Is that even a question to ask you since you abandoned us in the desert...?"

"I'm no monster," Tatiana replied, approaching Tristan with caution.

"It's hard to make that judgement after all that's happened. Then again, you did save my life, but you also aided terrorists destroy not one, but two world heritage sites. Imagine what future generations will think of people like you. Imagine what your own children would think of you. Do you have kids?"

Tatiana did not respond.

"No response tells me that you do. I'm sure they'd be ashamed of you if they knew what you were doing..."

Tatiana made her approach so that she was a foot from Tristan. Tristan noticed her hands trembling. She pointed the barrel to Tristan's forehead, causing him to close his eyes and turn his head away.

"You're a brave little boy. You're valiant – I'll give you that," Tatiana remarked.

"You don't have to kill me," Tristan said.

"I'm not going to kill you," she replied, causing Tristan to open his eyes.

"She better not or else I'm going to have to kill her," Charlemagne added, pointing his revolver behind Tatiana's light brown hair.

She jumped and stood straight.

"Put the gun down, Tatia. You're not a monster. I know you're not. Prove me right, please?" Charlemagne requested.

Tatiana trembled some more before she gently lowered her rifle.

"Tristan, get some ties from my backpack and get her tied up. Move your hands behind your back, my dear. I'm afraid this is the end of the adventure for you."

Tatiana came quietly and even knelt down. Charlemagne kept the revolver pointed as Tristan did what Charlemagne asked of him. After that was done, Charlemagne gave the revolver to Tristan and grabbed the assault rifle.

"Take her to the top, Tristan," Charlemagne said. "I'm going to go help Diana."

"Sure thing."

Charlemagne's ears pointed up as he heard some yelling and gunfire from nearby. He then looked back over to Tristan and Tatiana.

"Hurry, we don't have much time and we don't know what Attila is willing to do to Diana."

Diana continued slowly as the trail got narrower and less stable. He got through a wider section before he paused to notice it was a dead-end.

"Oh crap…" Diana whispered, looking down to notice Attila on his approach.

Diana began to breath faster as she looked over to the other side where the trail continued. She then looked behind herself with fear. She quickly looked to the side to notice the great height she was at before she took another step backwards to hug the wall.

"No, no, no…" Diana muttered, closing her eyes. "Not like this."

Diana opened her eyes and jumped as if she had just fallen asleep and woken up. She looked to her left and saw that the situation had flipped. The left was now a dead-end and the right continued upwards.

"Wait, what?" Diana questioned, looking around.

Attila arrived at the opposite side and began to fire his assault rifle at Diana, causing her to duck out of the way and continue.

"Come here, you little brat! It's just you and me now!" Attila shouted.

Diana ran up the last bit of the trail and arrived at the entrance of a tunnel that went towards a grotto inside. Likewise, Tristan came to the top of his trail with Tatiana and saw that he had arrived at a dead-end.

"What?" Tristan muttered to himself. "You've got to be kidding me."

Diana went down the narrow cavernous tunnel and arrived at a garden-like area where a medium-sized structure sat in the middle with a domed roof and pillared supports connected by white marble walls. A ram-like deity was carved above the entrance, but Diana didn't go inside. Instead, she went around to hide. She peaked around the corner and saw Attila arrive.

"Come out wherever you are, princess," Attila remarked.

Diana snuck back and tried to stay out of sight. She went around and looked hopeless. She began to make her way around to get inside the tomb when she closed her eyes again and kept her back to the wall. She started to shuffle only to notice that her feet were now on marble instead of grass. She staggered where she was and looked around with panic.

"What the hell is going on?" Diana whispered, looking around the tomb with all its treasures piled around.

A sarcophagus stood in the middle and over it was a golden flail. Diana quickly went over and grabbed the mace, and as soon as she grabbed it, she ran outside. She gritted her teeth and steadied her feet as she noticed Attila ahead, walking cautiously.

"Not outside, huh? Well, I guess I'll just have to smoke you out from inside," Attila said.

Diana tightened his grip around the flail and walked forward. She brought her hands back as the two of them arrived at the entrance of the tomb, but before she could whack Attila over the head with it, Charlemagne arrived and fired his gun.

The shot missed, but Attila lunged forward with his rifle and started to fire. Diana immediately swung the flail behind Attila's back, causing him to fall forward before she hit again and caused him to pass out.

Charlemagne looked out from the cover he had taken and then ran forward to assist Diana. Diana tossed the flail onto the ground and panted.

"Diana, are you alright?" Charlemagne questioned, bringing a hand to her shoulder.

"Yeah, I'm cool," Diana replied, looking down at Attila. "I'm fine."

Act 5, Scene 4

Charlemagne finished putting ties on Attila before he rushed into the tomb. Tristan arrived with Tatiana and Benito while Johnathan appeared with a bloodied shirt, Francisco and Gudrun. They were all set to sit down near the entrance. Johnathan was given an assault rifle to hold while Charlemagne searched around the tomb of Alexander the Great for the orb.

"What are you even looking for, Charles?" Francisco questioned.

"Never you mind," Charlemagne remarked, opening the sarcophagus with Tristan to see that it was empty.

Charlemagne looked surprised as he looked into the empty casket. He then stamped a foot and turned around.

"It's not here," Charlemagne said to Johnathan. "Damn!"

"What is not here?" Miklos questioned.

"Shut up!" Charlemagne yelled at him. "None of you are allowed to speak! None of you! I'm thoroughly and utterly disappointed in each and every single one of you for the things you have done, the people you have become, and what you have let happen! I taught you all better than this. I taught you all far better from this and you've all sunk well below my expectations. I think less of all of you for the actions you have taken.

"You cannot blame us, Charles. We were paid to do a job," Benito explained.

"I *can* blame you, because I had always taught you that this was never about money. Where were each and every one of you on the 29th of June this year? Not in Allabrese for sure. Our dear friend, Konstantin Sakharov, died three days before then and I did not see any of you at the funeral. Not one – not a single damn one of you, and why? Because you were all blinded by greed, blinded by lust – all for this stupid necklace, well guess what –

that necklace is in the hands of dangerous terrorists that will continue to and stop at nothing to destroy the rich and valuable history of this ancient land. You've all participated in one of the greatest crimes against humanity: the destruction of ancient culture."

Charlemagne paused for a moment. None of the crew dared to speak as Charlemagne calmed down.

"Konstantin was our friend... and he would have been torn to know how we've come against one another out of a minor payout. He may have been a demolitionist, but he understood his limits when it came to helping us get out of tricky situations. He knew that he'd rather take his own life than to let something of great value to the future generations to be destroyed. He taught us all the values of the past, to preserve. How ironic."

Miklos looked to the side with a scowl. Charlemagne looked at him intently.

"And you, Miklos... you were just an eager and young lad when I first met you. You told me that you wanted to see the world for all its riches and values You wanted to meet all sorts of people and to understand the other sides of the world. What happened to you?"

Charlemagne shook his head.

"I'm disappointed foremost by you, son. I'm disappointed in all of you..."

"I'm sorry, Charles," Tatiana came to say. "I'm sorry..."

"Don't be sorry to me, my dear," Charlemagne replied, shaking his head. "Be sorry for yourself."

Charlemagne took a deep breath and then looked over to Johnathan.

"Johnathan, is our transport on its way? Charlemagne questioned him.

"I'm not sure, sir. I'll keep an eye out to see." he replied

"Good, very good," Charlemagne said, looking over to the kids as they rested.

"Wait..." Francisco said, looking up and over to Charlemagne. "Why did you say that the terrorists have the necklace? I thought that was the reason we were here in the first place – to take it from you."

"What?" Charlemagne questioned, looking over to him. "What are you talking about? Are you not here for another reason? For this tomb?"

"What?" Benito asked. "No?"

The old crew started to mutter between them as Charlemagne looked at them with confusion.

"Hold up!" Charlemagne yelled. "What was your mission here? What did Ali al-Suli send you to do?"

"Our mission was to take the amulet from you – Doctor Vidkunsen confessed to giving it to you."

"What?" Charlemagne questioned.

"Perhaps I should explain..." Dr. Vidkunsen replied. "When you were at the temple, I felt bad for all that had happened and did not want the necklace to go into the hands of those terrorists. I had no idea we were aiding such sinister men, so when I had the chance, after Tristan had dropped the necklace to fight with Tanya, I took it and placed it in Diana's backpack. I then opened the briefcase and threw the false one onto the floor where Tristan dropped the former. With Diana's backpack, I ran after her so I could rescue her and give her backpack to her. Have you not noticed it with you?"

Diana froze and then brought her backpack around to check.

"I- I haven't checked my backpack with all that's happened. I didn't realize either," Diana confessed, opening it to reveal the necklace at the very bottom underneath all her things.

Diana grabbed the necklace by its chains. She quickly let go to bring it into the palm of her other hand by the orb.

"It's here!" Diana proclaimed. "Oh my God! Wait, this explains so much…"

"Explains what?" Tristan asked.

"The necklace!" Charlemagne said, going over and looking at it. "Johnathan, we've had it the whole time!"

Charlemagne laughed as Diana handed him the amulet. He took it in hand, weighed it and then showed the others. Diana stood up with a smile. Tristan too. Charlemagne then showed it to them and they looked at it.

"We did it," Charlemagne said to them. "We have the orb!"

Charlemagne gave the necklace back to Diana and then hugged the three of them.

Act 6, Scene 1

Charlemagne sat in a Mi-26 helicopter provided the Huntsman with his new team next to him and old team across from him. Mercenaries rode with them as they flew across the country towards a city on the Mediterranean coast, Alexandria. The helicopter began to make its descent towards an airfield near the city, lowering down before stopping.

Charlemagne exited the helicopter with the briefcase and the mercenaries led the old team out. Johnathan held another briefcase with the false necklace.

"Right, so now what?" Johnathan questioned, looking around as the sun set.

"Now, we hand this amulet to the right hands," Charlemagne replied.

"Absolutely, sir," Johnathan agreed. "So, should we work on getting transit back to the United Kingdom or Canada?"

"Not so hasty," Charlemagne reacted. "First, we must travel to the Sinai and deliver this to the *right* hands."

"You can't be serious, sir," Johnathan remarked. "You're going to deliver the amulet to the religious fool?"

"I made a promise, and after all that's happened, I would rather it be in their hands, resting in a vault somewhere than anywhere else. If there's one thing I've learned from our last adventure, it's that this necklace and orb draw the worst out of people's greed. Not to mention given the geopolitical circumstances, terrorists, this race and whatnot. It is better in the hands of people who knew where the amulet was and decided to leave it there."

Johnathan didn't reply.

"Besides, they told me they'd ship it to me for research at the right time, and that right time is not now. Right now, I need all this excitement to die down."

"And the replica?" Johnathan questioned.

"Even a replica of the amulet is too high profile – the simple-minded don't know the difference between the true amulet and its fakes. I'll have that returned to the priest as well."

"I see…" Johnathan replied, looking around.

Johnathan pointed out some mercenaries and whistled their attention. The mercs rushed forward and drew their weapons. Diana and Tristan watched as they left the helicopter and brought their hands up. The old team simply looked from where they stood nearby on the helipad, still in ties.

"I'm afraid I can't let that happen, sir," Johnathan said. "You might be my mentor, but I also take orders from Zimmerman and he would not want that necklace to be locked and forgotten."

"Johnathan, what are you talking about?" Charlemagne asked, looking over to the mercenaries and then his intern. "Don't make this mistake."

"I'm sorry, sir," Johnathan replied, taking the briefcase from his hand and then walking off.

"Oh, for God's sake," Charlemagne remarked.

"Come on, we're leaving!" Johnathan shouted, going to a jeep prepared for him.

Johnathan entered the jeep with the mercenaries. The jeep and the jeep behind it then drove off from the airfield. Two mercenaries remained with rifles pointed at Charlemagne and within range of firing at the kids. Tristan looked over to Attila as he looked at the two guards. He then whispered to Tatiana. Tristan frowned as they conspired. The two then rushed forward and snuck up behind each of the mercenaries before taking them down and disarming them. Charlemagne saw this and then took a deep sigh.

Diana and Tristan then lowered their hands. Tristan rushed forward and towards the edge of the helicopter landing zone, pointing to the convoy.

"We have to go after them!"

"What's the point…" Charlemagne replied. "We don't have the means to chase them right now."

Charlemagne and Tristan turned their attention to Attila who brought his thigh down to the neck of one of the mercenaries.

"Where did they take the amulet?!" Miklos shouted. "Answer me!"

"Get him off me!" the merc pleaded in his Russian accent.

Charlemagne's head spun as he saw Tatiana holding down the other guard. Dr. Vidkunsen rushed over to help her while Benito and Francisco secured the legs of the mercenary Attila was interrogating.

"Charles!" Tristan yelled. "They have two other jeeps!"

"I have keys here!" Tatiana added. "Let me go!"

Diana took a step forward, but then looked over to Charlemagne.

"The port! The port!" the mercenary cried out. "Just let me go!"

"You heard him," Miklos said to Charlemagne. "They're going to the port. Hurry if you want to catch them!"

Charlemagne didn't reply. He hesitated to move as he looked around.

"Charles, do you want to get that amulet back or just stand there? Hurry!"

"Why should I trust you?" Charlemagne replied.

"Charles, we don't have time to bicker!" Tatiana complained. "Let us redeem ourselves."

Charlemagne looked at her and then sighed.

"I'm a moron," he whispered, taking out a knife and going over to free her.

Tatiana then grabbed the assault rifle, kicked the mercenary in the side and ran to free Dr. Vidkunsen while Charlemagne freed Miklos, Benito and Francisco. Miklos searched the mercenary he was sat atop for keys and then knocked him out. He then grabbed the assault rifle and ran towards the other jeep. Tatiana started the first jeep and had Dr. Vidkunsen take the wheel.

"Where do we go?" Diana questioned to Charlemagne as she and Tristan arrived at the jeeps with him.

"Oh, just stay with Tanya," Charlemagne replied, entering Miklos' jeep. "Be safe."

"Yes, sir," Tristan replied, entering the first jeep.

Once they were aboard, Gudrun drove off at a high-speed and went along. Benito took control of the other jeep with Miklos in the front with him holding the assault rifle. Charlemagne and Francisco sat in the back. They then drove off behind the others.

Each of them sped forward and came onto the road of the Alexandrian countryside. Charlemagne held tightly as they dodged traffic to get a lead on the highway. Eventually, the two jeeps closed in on the jeeps ahead, alerting them and causing them to speed up.

"Cisco, take this," Miklos said, producing a pistol and handing it to him. "Lay down some fire with me."

"Yes, boss, but I won't be able to do much with one clip," Francisco replied, opening fire.

Charlemagne looked into the rear-view mirror as he saw the others behind them. He then looked ahead as one of the jeeps split up from the other.

"Where's Johnathan? I can't see him!" Charlemagne shouted. "They're splitting up!"

"I'll take the lead car," Benito remarked. "The others will know to take the other."

"Take the other," Tatiana shouted to Gudrun. "The others will take care of the other."

"Where am I going, Charles?" Benito questioned. "I need to know where this kid is going to get an advantage over him."

"The port is at the southside of the city. If you keep following him, that might be the best option," Charlemagne replied.

Benito complied.

"Alright, let's lay down some fire!" Attila shouted as he stood up with his assault rifle.

Attila opened fire with Francisco. The bullets bounced off the metal sides of the jeep, missing the tires. Francisco clicked the trigger and no more rounds came out.

"Pull up," Attila said, lowering the rifle. "I will board them."

"Are you mad?" Charlemagne questioned.

"No," Attila replied, looking to him. "It won't be the first time I've done this either."

Benito came up to the side of the jeep. Attila broke the glass atop his door and stood up. The other mercenaries looked at them with surprise. Benito attempted to stabilize the speed. The other jeep began to slow down.

"Easy," Attila warned Benito, "or I'll fall off!"

The driver of the jeep swerved into their jeep, causing Attila to fall into his seat. Charlemagne attempted to identity Johnathan among the troopers.

Tatiana found herself driving along the coast.

"Where are you going? You're letting them get away!" Tristan remarked.

"Don't you worry," Tatiana said. "Just hold on, put your seatbelt on and brace yourself."

Attila tried to adjust himself to stand up in the rear of the pickup truck, but the other jeep made it hard for him as it swerved into them again. Benito kept his distance some more before he decided to speed up again and hit the car in the rear. He then quickly swerved out of the way as the two of them nearly hit a large truck.

The two cars continued to race into the city when the jeep decided to take a turn left, catching Charlemagne off-guard.

"No…" he muttered as he quickly turned.

"There! I saw them make a right turn ahead!" Francisco observed.

"I have them!" Benito replied, speeding along.

The jeep they were chasing reunited with the other jeep.

"Where's Tatiana?" Charlemagne questioned, looking around as they caught up to the two cars.

One of the jeeps pulled back and began to drive into their jeep. Ahead of them was the shipping yard where a Zimmerman Corps. frigate was parked along the side of the harbor.

Out of the blue, the other jeep driven by Tatiana came out and rammed the jeep ahead in the side, causing it to spin out of control and hit the fence outside of the harbor. In this same moment, Benito drove their jeep into the side of the other jeep, causing it to hit a lamp post before they entered the shipping yard, each jeep stopping at where the fence was to stop them from escaping.

Miklos jumped out of the jeep and ran towards the wreckage, pulling Johnathan out and leaving a bloody trail behind him. The jeep shot up in smoke from where it lay on its side. The two briefcases had slid out and stopped across the harbor asphalt. Charlemagne got out of the vehicle with Tatiana and the others go over and surround Attila and Johnathan, but unbeknownst to them, mercenaries protecting the harbor reacted and closed in on them.

The Huntsman mercenaries shot their rifles into the air, causing the entire crew to duck down.

"Get off of him!" a mercenary shouted, pushing past Charlemagne to force Attila off from Johnathan who face was all bloodied.

Other mercenaries secured the briefcases, checking each one and then passing one to the other and the other to another. One of the briefcases was tossed to the squad leader, Kodiak, the young son of the commander.

Sirens could be heard in the distance and Charlemagne looked around to see that the mercs were pointing their weapons that them, ready to fire. They were surrounded. From their crouched positions, they brought their hands up in surrender.

Attila punched the mercenary who tried to stop him, requiring an entire squad to be sent to stun him with stun batons.

"Enough!" a man shouted from atop of the boat.

Charlemagne looked over to see Audric Zimmerman standing with two guards at his side. One of the guards being the scar-faced commander of the mercenaries. Charlemagne scowled at them. Audric walked along the side of the boat and down a ramp before joining everyone. Charlemagne watched as the commander yelled at his men in Russian and then backed off as police began to arrive. One of the briefcases was passed to Zimmerman who opened it, dipped his hands in and then nodded. He closed it and gave it to Kodiak to take with him.

The mercenaries lowered their guns and stopped electrocuting Attila.

"What is going on here?" a high-ranking police officer said, walking towards them as various tactical police officers surrounded them with assault rifles.

A mercenary gave another briefcase to Zimmerman and then backed off. The high-ranking officer walked over to Zimmerman and took the briefcase off him.

"Superintendent, I believe you are trespassing," Zimmerman stated to him. "I own this dock – this is private property."

"To hell with your property," the superintendent replied. "Are you the one responsible for the disruption in my city?"

"Surely not," Zimmerman replied with sarcasm. "Why would I, Audric Zimmerman of Zimmerman Corporation, be responsible for all this mayhem? I was inspecting this boat of mine when I heard all the commotion and asked myself the same question of 'What is going on?' Perhaps we should ask Mr. Charlemagne de la Cabernet what is going on – after all, it's his men who are bloodied and wailing on the floor."

"Shut up," the superintendent replied. "You are all under arrest."

"Now, now," Zimmerman reasoned. "Perhaps we can come to some sort of agreement, perhaps compensation for all this trouble."

Diana frowned at Zimmerman and shook her head. The officer looked back at Zimmerman without replying.

Act 6, Scene 2

"I can't believe he just paid them off," Diana replied. "Wait, no – I can believe it."

"Money does make the world go round," Tristan remarked.

The police left the port and the Huntsman were allowed to resume control of the harbor as they rounded up the crew. Charlemagne crossed his arms as Zimmerman approached him.

"I should have known you were behind all of this – the race, I mean," Charlemagne said to him. "I can't believe I let myself be betrayed by you as well – I trusted you and thought you were my friend!"

"Charles, you are my friend, but you're also my competition out here. I'm a businessman – this is what we do. I just paid out your bail and saved your from humiliation at the hands of the press. If you want to paint an enemy, the press is the enemy of us businessmen."

"It was you all this time. You set up the race. You dragged me into this race because you knew that I was the only one that would be able to solve the mystery of the amulet. You used me. These men... they're the same men from Russia. You sent them after me. You hired Allodia's boyfriend to spy on me and cause all the events that happened. I wouldn't be surprised if the mole in my tech company was one your agents as well, or worse, you."

"I can't believe these accusations from you, Charles," Zimmerman replied. "Perhaps this heat is getting to you."

"Oh, shut up," Diana barked at him. "The Huntsmen are your private army. We know the truth."

Zimmerman put his hands into his pockets and smiled at Diana. He then looked over to Tristan with a frown and then back over to Charlemagne.

"Charles, you and your friends are free to go. I'll be taking the real necklace of the Son of Ra into the care of Zimmerman Technologies. I'm really sorry you feel this way about me, but you have a misunderstanding I believe. Besides, I think it's time you get an army of yourself if you believe what you believe. Of course, that wouldn't be good PR for you, would it?"

"Wait until the board of directors hears about this," Charlemagne replied. "There'll be a unanimous vote in favor of your removal."

"Yes, I suppose we'll just have to wait for that," Zimmerman replied with a frown. "Naturally, I'd offer you voyage back to Harlech with me to celebrate our success, but I can see you're a little agitated. I'll leave you be with your friends."

Charlemagne didn't respond.

"Right, well, I'll see you at the next meeting later this month, Charles. Safe journey home," Zimmerman said in slight sarcasm before walking off.

Diana continued to frown at him. The remaining mercenaries escorted them off the property and onto the streets of Alexandria.

"What a load of crap!" Diana shouted. "I can't believe this – after all this trouble, we let ourselves be played by that smug son of a bitch!"

"Now there, Diana. Calm down," Charlemagne said to her. "Not all is lost."

Diana frowned at him. Charlemagne walked over to Tristan and Diana and put a shoulder on each of them.

"Children, the adventure we just shared was a mighty one, one that I'm sure you'll both remember with strong details, but it just goes to show that not all of them end up as you expect – with treasure in hand. For me, I'm simply glad that the two of you are safe, and that the panic and fear is over. Zimmerman is not the worst person whose hands could be around that amulet…remember that. After all, while must has been destroyed, including at my own hand, a lot has been uncovered in its place. We documented the secret tomb of Hatshepsut's heir with your camera and we also uncovered a tomb belonging to Alexander the Great. We've made history in these short weeks."

"But how do we know that people will believe us?" Tristan questioned. "I mean, the Egyptian government was so comfortable keeping so much that we had uncovered hidden. History won't be written as it should, truthfully."

"No…" Charlemagne sighed. "You're right, but that goes to show something you should both know. History is never written exactly as it should. History is never written in exact details of the past. We can never know exactly how life was in ancient times. For all we know, everything we surmise of ancient Egypt is false and an over-estimation on our parts due to our expectations and biases. History is simply our interpretation and attempt to understand what occurred, and there are more sinister people who will manipulate that for their own gain, but there are also others who pursue truth. Truth is what matters. Even in our recent history, there are dark chapters that are difficult to understand and ones that we might never know what happened because of lack of evidence. History should strive for truth and only truth. A realist knows that history is full of holes and forged information. It's someone else's interpretation."

Tristan looked at Charlemagne and nodded. Diana frowned and looked to the side.

"Charles?" Miklos questioned.

"Yes?" Charlemagne questioned, turning to face him.

"I'm sorry for all the harm I have done to you and your family. I have allowed greed to consume me, and I drove my wife into that same path. I forgot what I stood for and became more animal than the man you made me into. Please, I beg your forgiveness."

"Me too," Tatiana replied from behind.

"I do too," Benito said.

"As do I," Francisco said.

"And I as well," Dr. Vidkunsen affirmed. "Sakharov would truly have been ashamed with all of us, and I am most of all saddened that I disgraced him by choosing to be here rather than at his funeral to bid him farewell."

Charlemagne looked at his old friends and nodded.

"Nevermind that. Sakharov would have wanted us to be here together. Sakharov would be proud that you all came through in the end and we worked as a team. I certainly am proud and grateful. So, if you'll forgive me for my mistakes, I can certainly forgive yours."

"Yes," Attila replied. "Thank you, Charles."

Charlemagne smiled and laughed. He extended his hand to his old friend.

"It's in the past now," Charlemagne said.

Miklos took Charlemagne's hand and hugged him. He then patted him on the back and they parted.

"I'm sure you're all exhausted, but how about we all dine out one last time for old time's sake?" Charlemagne requested. "Come, let us go and relax."

Epilogue

"I still can't believe Zimmerman ended up paying less than fifty million in that bribe he offered," Diana pouted with crossed arms.

"I'm just glad that it's all over," Tristan replied, resting his head to the side of Diana's chair.

The two of them were sat together on a commercial flight home. Charlemagne took the aisle seat and was reading a British newspaper.

"I'm glad that Egyptian authorities managed to wrap up the crisis before it got out of hand. Hundreds of suspected extremists were arrested in connection to the Brethren of Islam in Egypt. It's eased my conscience about this whole ordeal," Charlemagne said.

"What do you think happened to Ali?" Tristan asked.

"Al-Suli?" Charlemagne questioned, lowering his paper. "I have no idea. I haven't thought about him. "I'm sure he's fine, but I'll tell you what. What I can't get my mind off of is why Zimmerman wanted that amulet. He didn't strike me as a collector."

"Do you think he knows about the myth around it?" Diana asked.

"I doubt it, and for that, I am okay with him having the necklace. I could not have lived with knowing that Ali al-Suli had the necklace or those terrorists. It bothers me to know that others won't be able to enjoy the relic, but as long as it is in secured hands, I'm fine."

"Yeah, it's just a necklace after all," Tristan replied, yawning.

"Of course…" Charlemagne replied, looking aside.

"Right…" Diana added, looking out the window again. "It's just an ordinary necklace.

"In all that's happened, I suppose I should also be glad that you kids are safe. I over-extended myself on this journey and did not intend for you to go through all that you did. I hope you can forgive me on that."

"It's no problem, Charles," Tristan replied.

"Yeah, no problem at all," Diana agreed.

Diana looked out the window and into the dusk outside as the sun finished setting. The skies were clear over the water and the stars shined through. Darkness extended over.

"You know, there was an ancient Egyptian tale about nightfall," Charlemagne said, looking out the window with the kids. "They said that every night, Ra left to go slay a snake demon Apep. His return in the form of the morning signaled his triumph. Some Egyptians believed in this so much that they feared mornings where the sun didn't rise, because it signaled that Ra had fallen."

"I really liked Egypt," Diana said with a warm smile. "It's too bad we couldn't stay longer."

"Yes, it's quite the unfortunate turn of events," Charlemagne replied, flicking through his newspaper as he went back to reading.

Tristan turned his head to look out the window with Diana. The two of them wrapped their hands underneath the blanket they shared.

Suddenly, a flick of light streaked across the night sky.

"Make a wish…" Tristan muttered.

"I wish we could go home already," Diana remarked. "This flight is taking forever."

"What a boring wish," Tristan replied.

"Sue me."

"History is the version of past events that people have agreed upon."

– Napoleon Bonaparte